Ghost Soldiers

9-9-17

Esther,

Happy Reading!

[illegible]

Amanda Bonn[illegible]

Also By Shawn Settle

The Hallie McKinley Series

Book 1: Trust Me

Ghost Soldiers

By Shawn Settle

Illustrated By Amanda Bonner

www.shawnsettle.com

This book is a work of fiction. Places, characters, names, and incidents either are products of the author's imagination or are used fictitiously. Any resemblance to actual events or persons, living or dead, is entirely coincidental.

ISBN-10: 154817050X
ISBN-13: 978-1548170509

Special thanks to my dad for all his help in ensuring the accuracy of the story. I had a lot of fun working on this project with you.

Dedicated to all U.S. service men and women, and to their families, for all the sacrifices you've made for our country.

Chapter 1

1979, Venice Beach, California

Here he was again, staring through his binoculars checking out a potential client. As he reflected back over his life, it wasn't supposed to go this way. He was a Lieutenant in the Army, well at least he had been until the government brought him home from war, and then charged him, and two of his buddies, with treason. His best friend, Billy Baxter, went crazy and was put in the psychiatric ward of the V.A. Hospital in Los Angeles. His commanding officer, Rick Peters, and he were felons, wanted by the U.S. Army and living on the run. It had been nine years. Nine years of always looking over his shoulder. Nine years of living as a mercenary for hire, helping people. Yes, they were picky about who they worked for. They only helped the disadvantaged, the underdog, the ordinary person who was just trying to make it in the world and who was being harassed, bullied. That wasn't all they did, there was the occasional rescuing of a kidnapped person and other random assignments. Whatever needed to be done to make money to live off of, but one day, one day he wanted to just settle down, to stop being on the run, to live a normal life, maybe have a wife and kids.

"Do you see anything?" His thoughts were

interrupted by the Major.

"Nope. She's sitting on the bench like Mrs. Jones told her to."

This potential client was more of an unusual case. She had come to Billy looking for them. He knew her as Sam. She was a regular visitor at the V.A., knew most of the patients, and if you asked them about her, they would tell you that she was an "angel who saved their life." Billy didn't know exactly what they meant, but he got the impression they would do anything for her. Billy had talked to her on numerous occasions, said she was a sweet, loving kid. When she had come to him asking for them, he was surprised she knew of the connection. They couldn't be too careful of a military plant trying to find them, so Billy told her he didn't know them, but he'd heard rumors that Mrs. Jones could get in touch with them.

Rick had watched as Mrs. Jones asked Sam the questions he was feeding her through an ear mic. Sam was 22-years-old and looking for a friend of hers, Joe Simon, a Vietnam vet. The guys had a soft spot in their hearts for vets, since they were vets themselves. There hadn't been a lot of information to go on. Sam didn't know what trouble Simon might be in, just that he hadn't called her and she considered him missing. Sam was very worried about him and willing to pay $10,000 to find him. The entire story sounded suspicious. Rick had even commented that surely Col. Walters could come up with a better story than that. No, normally they wouldn't consider taking a case like this, but Billy wanted to help her, to at least check into her story.

So here they were, down by the beach, waiting and watching to see if she was being tailed by the military.

"Rick, she's got some company." Mark watched through the binoculars as four guys in their twenties walked up to the jet black-haired, white girl sitting on the bench. She didn't look like she belonged at the beach. It was a beautiful, sunny day, nice and warm. Everyone else was in swimsuits or at least shorts. This kid was sitting on the bench in jeans and a long sleeved, plaid shirt. She wore sneakers and had a backpack strapped to her back. "They appear to be giving her a hard time."

"Patience, Mark. If she gets into serious trouble, we'll jump in and help her. We have to make sure she's not a bird dog for the military."

Mark watched as one of the guys grabbed her by the arm. She kneed him in the groin, causing him to let go; she ran for it. "They're chasing her down the beach. She's a pretty fast runner... She's run onto the pier."

"That's an interesting move." Rick commented.

"Yeah, maybe she thinks one of the fishermen will help her."

"What's happening now?"

"She's come to the end of the pier. Rick, they have her trapped. Don't you think we should step in and help?"

"Patience, Lieutenant. They'll have to bring her back down the pier to take her off. We don't need to get caught on the end of a pier with nowhere to go."

"I don't believe it." Mark commented at what he

was watching. "She has climbed up on the railing of the pier. She just waved 'good-bye' to the goons and did a backflip off the pier into the water."

"What? Let me see those binoculars."

Mark handed the binoculars to him and just sat there, stunned. He'd never seen anything like it. The kid was either gutsy or as crazy at Billy, maybe a little bit of both.

"I found her. She's surfaced by the pilings."

"What is she doing now?"

"It looks like she's hiding and waiting. Mark, this isn't your average kid. I have a strange feeling about her. Normal kids don't jump off piers and hide the way she is." Rick handed the binoculars back to him.

Mark found her hanging on as the waves knocked her against the pilings. "This reminds me of when we used to hide from Charlie in the rivers."

"It looks like she knows what she's doing."

"Yeah, but the question is, is she really military? She hangs around the V.A. a lot, it's possible one of the vets could have told her stories of things we did in Nam. Billy believes her and wants to help her."

"I know, which is the only reason we're not leaving right now. Let's keep watching and see what happens next."

It was about an hour before she moved from her position. She slowly made her way from piling to piling until she was at the shore. Mark watched as she cautiously snuck her way up the beach underneath the pier. She was looking and watching. She was also grabbing her left shoulder, it was obvious she had hurt it. He wanted to tell her that the guys who were chasing her were long gone; they had taken off the moment she'd jumped off the pier.

He watched her look around again and then suddenly stand up, walk up the beach like nothing was going on, like she wasn't fully clothed and dripping wet. "She's on the move. I'm going to follow her." Mark handed Rick the binoculars, jumped out of the van, and followed the kid into a beach shop.

Mark discretely spied on her. He watched her pick out a shirt, a white cotton blouse with long sleeves. She also picked out some jeans that were three-quarters, some sandals, and a hairdryer. He moved over close to her and then bumped into her left shoulder. She winced in pain and grabbed it. He hadn't bumped her that hard. "I'm sorry. I didn't see you there."

"Don't worry about it." She looked up and her deep blue eyes caught his attention.

"Are you okay? You seem to be in pain."

"I'm fine. I was in an accident a couple of days ago. I'm just a bit bruised and sore. Don't worry about it. It's nothing, really."

"That's an interesting fashion statement you're making." Mark glanced down at her wet clothes.

"Uh, yeah." She sheepishly smiled. "I unexpectedly went swimming."

She then walked away from him and toward the cash register. Mark got in line behind her. The cashier was talking to two children, telling them they didn't have enough money for what they were trying to buy.

Sam spoke up, "Here. I have it." She offered to pay the difference due. Mark watched her swing the backpack off her shoulder and pull out some money. She then paid for her items as well. Mark noticed, despite the fact she was dripping wet, all the bills she pulled out of the dark green backpack were dry. She asked where the ladies room was located and proceeded to walk over to it and go inside.

Mark watched the door and waited. He could hear the hair dryer running and figured she was getting cleaned up. It took her about half-an-hour, but when she finally emerged, he had to do a double take. He couldn't believe his own eyes. A beautiful lady with golden, blonde hair came out of the bathroom. It was the same clothes, same backpack, same five-footish frame, but she looked totally different. Mark discretely looked into the bathroom to confirm that there was only a toilet and sink, no window, no way she could be a different person. He watched from afar as she picked out a straw hat and some sunglasses. One thing was for sure, she now looked like she belonged at the beach and would not stick out like she had before.

Mark followed her out of the shop and watched as she walked back down the beach to sit on the bench. He went back to the van.

"I'm telling you, Rick; that is the girl."

"Mark, that girl has blonde hair, the girl we're looking for has black hair."

"If I hadn't been watching her, I wouldn't have believed it either. But I'm telling you, it's the same girl. There's no way the military can be following her, she looks completely different."

"We can't be too cautious. Maybe Walters knows what she looks like in this disguise. Aren't you a bit nervous that she even has her own disguise? It also bothers me that we ran her prints and all the computer came up with is Samantha Anderson, age 22 from Peaceville, Georgia. Don't you find it a bit strange that there was no information about where she was born, there are no school records? Even the name of the town she's from sounds suspicious. Billy says she's at the V.A. every couple of months. If she lives in Georgia, then what's she doing at the V.A. in Los Angeles every couple of months? It doesn't add up. We're going to wait and watch a bit longer. We can't be too careful."

Mark sat back in his seat and went back to watching her with his binoculars. The afternoon wore on. At one point, she got up, walked over to a food vendor, bought a hamburger and drink, then walked back to the bench to sit and eat. She just stared at the ocean. He wondered what she was thinking about.

The sun set. Rick was ready to test her one more time. He was dressed in a police officer's uniform and was wearing a microphone, so Mark could hear the conversation. There was a big, beautiful full moon, so they could see fairly well, too.

"Young lady, I'm going to have to ask you to leave this beach."

"Why?" She looked over at him.

"Because, it's after dark and no one can be on the beach after dark, so move along." Rick motioned for her to get.

"With all due respect, sir, it isn't a crime to sit at the beach after dark."

"Well, young lady. It seems you're

argumentative. I'm going to need to see your ID."

Mark watched as she reached into the backpack and pulled out her license. He heard Rick read. "Samantha Anderson, age 22 from Peaceville, Georgia. California's a long way from Georgia. What are you doing here?"

"Visiting some friends."

"I see, have you always lived in Georgia?"

"No, sir, I'm an orphan. I've moved around a lot." That caught Mark's attention. He was an orphan as well. He knew what that life was like.

"So, if I call in, am I going to find out all this information?"

"I don't know what you'll find or what you're getting at. If you're asking if I have a criminal record, the answer is 'no'."

Rick walked over to sit next to her. "Why are you sitting on this bench?"

"I'm waiting for some friends."

"When are they coming?"

"I'm not sure, but I told them I'd wait here for them to arrive."

"What if they don't come tonight?"

She smiled. "Then I guess I'm going to sit on this bench all night."

"And what mischief will you get into while you stay on the beach all night? I can't allow this."

"You don't have to worry about me, officer. I'll just sit here and think."

"And what exactly will you be thinking about? Causing mischief?"

"You're not a very trusting person, are you?"

"I don't trust kids. They're hoodlums. They cause all sorts of trouble everyday down here at the beach. So what are you really doing down here? Who are these people you are meeting?"

"Look, if you don't mind, I would like to just sit here and think and wait for my friends. There is no law against that."

"Look here, Missy. I am the law, and if I say you can't stay on the beach tonight, then you can't stay."

"You seem like a nice man, and I understand your issue with hoodlums; I ran into some of them myself a bit earlier today. However, I'm just sitting here, thinking while I wait. There's no law against that."

"What are you thinking about?"

"My brother." Mark noticed there was a sudden distance in her tone.

"Is your brother meeting you tonight?"

"No sir, he died ten years ago. He never saw a beach or ocean. He would have loved it. Look, I appreciate that you are doing your job, but I'm not a problem and the people I'm meeting are Vietnam veterans. They aren't kids or hoodlums. They made great sacrifices to give us the freedoms we enjoy living in the U.S. like the freedom to sit on the beach at night. I promise you there won't be any mischief here."

"Aren't you a bit young to have friends who are Vietnam vets?"

She smiled. "Like I said, I'm an orphan. You could say my entire adopted family is made up of Vietnam vets."

"Well, Missy, in that case, I want to tell you

congratulations. You've found who you're looking for. I'm Major Rick Peters."

Sam looked at Rick. "It's nice to finally meet you. I need your help."

Since Sam was a regular at the V.A., Mark got her to help him spring Billy the following morning. He enjoyed running the scam with her. She seemed to be a natural at it. Mark also noticed that she seemed to be more relaxed once Billy joined the group.

Sam told them that Simon moved around a bit. She figured another friend of hers, Chris Anthony, would know where Simon was currently living. However, she couldn't reach him. Anthony was a park ranger at Lassen Volcanic National Park, so they started heading north.

The beginning of the nine hour drive was filled with Billy and Sam talking. They got along really well. Mark was amazed that no matter what crazy, off the wall thing Billy said, Sam went right along with it. There was something special about the way they interacted, like they were on a unique level all their own. Mark was happy for his best friend. Billy was a bit crazy, but he had a really good heart. It was nice to see someone accept him for who he was and not treat him like he was crazy.

They stopped to get gas. While getting back into the van, Sam bumped her left shoulder causing her to wince in pain and drop to her knees.

Mark could tell from the look of Billy's face, he

was worried about her. "What's wrong with your shoulder?"

"It's nothing. I'm fine."

"What's wrong with your shoulder? Let me see it."

"It's fine, really. I was in an accident a couple of days ago. There's nothing to see; just some bad bruises."

"Maybe we should stop and have a doctor take a look at it."

"Billy, I'm fine, really. I've already had a doctor look at it. He gave me some pain medicine, but I haven't taken it, because it makes me sleepy. I have to find Simon."

Billy started moving things around the back of their van. "It's going to be several more hours before we reach the park. Here, I've made you a bed on the backseat. Take your pain medicine. I'll wake you when we start getting close."

Sam smiled at him. "Thanks, Billy."

The pain medicine seemed to really knock her out. She didn't even budge when they stopped for gas again. She was sleeping on her stomach. Billy put a blanket on her.

They weren't far down the road when she started talking in her sleep. The first sentence out of her mouth was so surprising, the entire team turned around to look at her.

Chapter 2

"Did I just hear what I thought I heard?" Mark asked them.

"She's speaking Vietnamese." Rick answered. "How does a 22-year-old white girl from Georgia know how to speak fluent Vietnamese? I keep telling you guys, I've got a weird feeling about this kid."

Sam kept speaking in her sleep. Mark tried hard to make out what she was saying. It had been nine years since he'd been stationed in Vietnam. He was a bit rusty with the language.

The team could make out that she was trying to stop someone from doing something. Her sleep was getting more and more agitated, the sentences more and more alarmed. Billy moved to the back of the van, rolled her over onto her back, and started trying to wake her up. Eventually she screamed and woke herself up. Her eyes were wild and crazy, her hands were shaking. Billy grabbed her and hugged her, holding her tightly. "It's alright. Everything's going to be alright. Billy's not going to let anything hurt you." Billy gave the team a concerned look as he held her and talked to her. "You're going to be okay. Try taking some deep breaths."

Mark could tell that Billy understood what was happening, but for Mark, it didn't make any sense. It had been four years since the Vietnam War had pretty much ended. This kid would have only been eighteen, and she definitely wasn't Vietnamese. Mark was starting to agree with Rick. Things weren't adding up, maybe this was an elaborate trick by Walters.

Mark heard Sam tell Billy she was alright and she thanked him for helping her. She then asked how close they were to the National Park.

"Sam, you want to explain to me how a kid your age knows how to speak Vietnamese?" Rick inquired.

"What?" Sam game him a baffled look.

"Look, kid. I'm not in the mood for games. You either answer my question, or we'll stop this van right now and leave you by the side of the road."

Billy then added. "You were speaking Vietnamese in your sleep."

Sam looked down at the floor and then back up at Rick. "Yes, I speak Vietnamese. I told you; I'm an orphan. Some of my closest friends are Vietnamese refugees."

Mark looked at her, trying to figure her out. "You were having quite the nightmare. What were you dreaming about?"

She looked directly at him and softly said, "Something I don't want to remember, something too horrible to share."

Billy hugged her. "It's okay. Don't worry about it." He then proceeded to change the subject and the two of them started chatting like they had done the beginning of the trip.

Billy seemed to just dismiss what had happened, but Mark couldn't shake the strange feeling he now had about Sam.

Near Lassen Volcanic National Park, California

When they got close to the park, Sam started giving directions to Anthony's house. It was located down a windy, dirt road. Mark noticed there were a lot of fallen trees including a place where a tree had fallen across the road and had been cut just enough for one vehicle to fit through. The team went on alert. A park ranger was still the police; it was risky interacting with them. When they arrived at the end of the road, Mark noticed there was a tree that had fallen on the two-story house. The tree branches were tangled in the telephone lines.

They all got out of the van. Rick and Mark hung back as Sam walked up to the door and rang the bell. A few moments later, a lanky, white man around his early thirties answered. What took place next baffled him.

"Hi LT." Sam cheerfully greeted him.

"Dear God, Sam." He grabbed her in his arms and gave her a long, tight embrace. Tears welled up in his eyes, and he kissed her forehead. Mark couldn't remember when he'd last seen such a heartfelt embrace. "I heard about what happened. Are you okay, kid?"

"I'm fine, LT."

"Are you sure you're alright?"

She pulled back a little ways from his embrace and looked him in the eyes. "Hey, I'm fine, really. Don't worry, LT."

"I always worry about you. I have ever since that day you paid the price for my mistake." He had a look of remorse on his face.

"That was a very, long time ago. You need to forgive yourself." She gave him a kiss on the cheek.

He smiled at her.

Sam made the introductions, telling Anthony they were friends of hers and that they were looking for Simon. They were all invited into the house.

Anthony turned to Sam, "When's the last time you ate? Are you hungry?"

"No, I'm good. We ate not too long ago."

Mark watched them, trying to figure out their exact relationship. It was odd she was calling him LT. That's what he was called when he was in Nam.

"Why are you looking for Simon?" Anthony asked her.

"He didn't call in."

Anthony nodded his head and lit up a cigarette. "He moved to Reno a couple of weeks ago. I think he's staying with Carter while he finds a place of his own. You should be resting, not chasing after Simon. Simon can take care of himself."

"He's in trouble, LT. I can feel it."

Mark looked around the room and saw pictures of Anthony with his war buddies. He'd been a Lieutenant in the Army, just like Mark. There were also pictures of him with Sam when she was younger.

Rick was asking Anthony questions about Simon. Mark was half listening as he looked around the room, studying the pictures.

Anthony suddenly caught his attention. "Oh no! She's on the roof." He was on his feet and hurrying out the front door. Mark realized that he could hear a chainsaw. He looked around the room and was surprised he didn't see Sam. He didn't even know when she had left.

Outside, Anthony was calling up to her. "Sam, get off the roof. You know I hate it when you climb on roofs."

"I'm just cutting this tree off your house. I'm not going to fall."

"I've seen you fall; and it scared the crap out of me." His tone was filled with concern.

"That's only because the building collapsed. You don't expect your house to fall down, do you?" She continued removing the tree limbs.

"It makes me very nervous seeing you up there."

"I know. That's why I decided it would be better to ask for forgiveness than permission. There's no reason you should have to wait for someone to do this for you, when I can do it." She shot him a smile. "I'm almost done, then I'll come down."

A few minutes later, she used a rope to lower down the chainsaw. Mark looked around and realized he didn't see a ladder. He also noticed she was barefoot. How had she gotten up there? He watched as Sam wrapped the rope around the brick chimney and repelled off the house. Anthony caught her in his arms when she got down. "What am I going to do with you, kid?"

"Forgive me?" Sam smiled at him.

Anthony kissed her forehead. "Yeah. Go see if the phone's back up. If it is, I want you to call Jack. I'm sure he's worried sick about you."

Rick picked back up with his conversation with Anthony. "So, you're not convinced Simon is actually in trouble?"

"No." Anthony replied. "Look, I'd bet my life on Sam's gut instincts, but the anniversary of her brother's death is the day after tomorrow. She doesn't handle the day well, and she's been doing some strange things lately. I just don't know if Simon's really in trouble or if she's just being hyper sensitive given the date. What I can tell you, is that when Sam decides she's going to do something, there's no stopping her. I'm glad she's brought some friends along with her. I don't want her to be alone."

Sam walked outside carrying a handgun. "Hey, LT, can I borrow this?"

"Sure."

"I'm taking these two extra clips as well. Is that alright?"

"No problem."

"Thanks." She smiled tucking the gun into the back of her jeans. "I think we're all set. We need to hit the road if we are going to Reno today." Sam looked directly at Anthony. "I'm going to find Simon and bring him home."

"I know you will." Mark didn't miss the serious intensity of their exchange. "And Sam, do me a favor."

"What's that?"

"Don't kill anyone."

She smiled at him and gave a little laugh. "Don't worry, LT. I won't."

The good-bye exchange between them was as heartfelt as the hello. Anthony held her in his arms. "Stay safe, Sam. I love you, kid."

"I love you too, LT."

"Here," He reached into his pocket and pulled out his wallet. "Here's some money in case you need it. Next time, I'd love it if you came to stay for several days."

"I'll do that. Thanks again. I'll see you soon."

"See you soon, kid."

As they drove away, Mark commented. "He seems like a really nice guy."

"LT's the best." She smiled.

"You seem to be very close."

"We are."

"How long have you known him?"

"Just over ten-years. I met him not long after my parents died."

She then got really quiet. Mark could tell she was deep in thought.

They were traveling down highway three-ninety-five when they noticed a roadblock up ahead. All of a sudden, there was a military police car behind them with the lights flashing and the siren wailing.

Chapter 3

"How did Walters find us here?" Mark scowled as he slowed down the van. "They've got us boxed in, Rick."

"Lieutenant, drive right up to that road block and stop. Colonel Walters will let you pass." Sam was suddenly giving orders and braiding up her hair.

"Now, why would Walters do that?" Rick questioned while giving her a look of disbelief.

"Because Major, you're under my protection." Sam then turned back to Mark. "Lieutenant, can I borrow your vest?" She turned to Billy. "Captain, can I borrow your hat?"

"How do you know our ranks? Who exactly are you?" Rick was questioning Sam.

Sam was busy putting on the clothes she was borrowing. She then reached down into her pants and pulled out a pair of dog tags. Mark couldn't believe it.

"Look Major, we don't have time for me to answer questions. We also don't have time for Walters. We have to find Simon." She then turned to Billy. "Do you trust me, Captain?"

Mark watched as Billy nodded his head. "Yeah, I do."

"I promise you, Walters won't touch them."

"Rick!" Mark yelled. "They're closing in fast. What do you want me to do?"

From the look on Rick's face, he was as uncomfortable about this as Mark was. This was crazy. Drive right up to Walters and be allowed to pass. There was no way that was going to happen. Walters hated them and had been trying to arrest them for several years now. Mark figured hunting them down and arresting them seemed to be Walters's only job in the Army. Boy was he going to smirk with joy at capturing them today.

"We have limited options right now." Rick said. "Try it Sam's way." He then turned to Sam. "If you've double crossed us, kid…"

"Save your breath, Major." Sam interrupted him. "Now listen, the three of you need to stay in the van. Walters doesn't know Billy is part of the team. Let's keep that a secret. Put your windows down, so you can hear my conversation."

Mark pulled the van to a stop a few yards from the roadblock. Sam opened the sliding door and got out. Her shoulder length hair was completely hidden under Billy's blue baseball cap. Mark's cream vest, while being a little big, somehow suited her. The silver dog tags hung from her neck. She walked with a very confident stride over to Walters.

"Lieutenant Colonel Walters stand down your men." She ordered with a very firm tone.

Walters just laughed. "And who exactly are you supposed to be?"

"I'm General Sam Anderson, U.S. Marines, Special Forces."

Walters still looked amused. "Yeah right. Peters," Walters called over to them. "This is an absurd plan even for you. Now you and Luce get out of the van. You are both under arrest."

"That van and the men inside are under my command. We are on a top secret government mission and you, sir, are blowing my cover and slowing down my time table. Your insubordination will not go unnoticed. I will have you pushing paperwork for the remainder of your military career, if you don't let us pass." Sam barked at him.

Walters just laughed at her. "You expect me to believe you. You're just a kid. You have no authority over me. I work for the Pentagon."

"Call the Pentagon, ask to speak to General Wentworth. He will confirm I am telling the truth."

"Alright, I'll call your bluff, kid. When I'm done speaking to Washington, I'm going to arrest you and them." Walters turned to one of the men standing next to him. "Sergeant, get the Pentagon on the phone. Ask to speak to a General Wentworth."

Rick was grinning. "Well, you have to admit. The kid has spunk."

A few minutes later, Walters hung up the phone and immediately saluted Sam. "General Anderson, ma'am, please excuse me for not recognizing you."

Sam saluted him back. "You know, Colonel, it really bothers me that you are wasting taxpayer dollars chasing these men. Lieutenant Tom Mags massacred an entire village of civilians in Vietnam. That was a war crime. Punishing him was worth the taxpayer's money. These men gave classified documents to the enemy by accident. It was the middle of a war; miscommunications happened. I've read your service records, Colonel. I'm not very impressed with how you conduct yourself. Now, get these cars out of the middle of the road. Right now!"

"Yes, ma'am. Corporal, Captain, move those cars."

"Now Colonel, if I see you again or if you interfere with my mission in any way, I'll bury you. Am I making myself clear?"

"Yes, ma'am. Loud and clear." Walters saluted Sam again.

She returned the salute and motioned for Mark to move the van forward.

Rick laughed. "I love seeing Walters squirm." He smiled and waved at Walters as the van drove past him. "Hi Walters, better luck next time."

Once they were on the other side of the MP cars, Mark stopped to let Sam get back inside and then headed down the road. Sam removed the clothes she had borrowed, thanked them, and then tucked her dog tags in under her shirt, so they couldn't be seen.

Rick pulled a gun on her. "Billy."

Billy reluctantly grabbed the gun tucked into the back of her pants.

"Okay, kid, who are you, really?" Rick inquired.

"Put the gun away, Major." Sam calmly told him. "You're not going to kill me."

"What makes you so sure?"

"Because I've read all of your records. You aren't murderers. I highly doubt you're going to start being one today, especially since Walters can't touch you if you're with me."

"That doesn't mean I can't shoot you or break every bone in your body. Who are you, kid? I don't like being lied to."

"First, let's get one thing clear. There is nothing you can do to me to get me to tell you anything I don't want to tell you. Second, I have only told you the truth." To Mark's surprise, Sam started unbuttoning her shirt. "Billy, can you help me get this shirt off?"

"Sure thing."

"You know me, you all know me. You just don't remember me. Remember back to the days when you were POWs in Vietnam. One day, a kid came into the camp. It was a poor orphaned kid, begging for food. The NVA soldiers beat her around a bit and teased her. Later that night, that same kid brought you knives to cut the ropes off your wrists and ankles. That kid opened the locks to your cells and led you safely out of the prison camp and to the American troops who were waiting not far from the prison."

Mark tried hard not to remember being a POW, but as she described the night they were rescued, the memories came back. "How do you know this?"

Sam smiled at him. "I was that kid, Lieutenant."

"No way, how is that possible?"

She turned around. "Take a look at my back. Take a look at my arms. I know you recognize the scars. They are scars you don't get growing up in America. Lift the bandage covering my left shoulder. You'll see that I was shot two days ago, while on a mission to rescue American POWs who are still in Southeast Asia. So, yes, I am a general, and yes, I am only twenty-two. I am a classified government asset."

"If you are classified, why tell us?" Rick inquired.

"You already know me. It's technically not classified information to you."

"All those vets at the V.A. who say you are an angel who saved their lives," Billy asked. "Are they soldiers you rescued?"

"Yes."

"Are we really on a top secret government mission?" Rick asked her.

"No, that was just a lie I told Walters. I'm on my own time right now."

"But Walters called the Pentagon."

"Yes, and he asked for my commanding officer. General Wentworth knows I'm looking for Simon. He'll back up anything I say or do. Look, I hired you, because you are some of the best. My own unit would've helped, but I'm not on a government mission, and we got hit pretty hard the other day. They are all recovering. I can't do this on my own with a hole in my shoulder. Will you please help me find Simon and bring him home?"

"Yeah, kid. We'll help you." As Rick spoke the words, Billy helped her put her shirt back on.

Mark had so many questions he wanted to ask her, but before he could, she asked, "Hey, you guys like music?"

"Yeah!" Billy replied.

Sam pulled out a harmonica and started playing.

Billy asked, "Where'd you learn to play?"

She smiled. "When I met the Sarge, he was learning. He taught me what he knew and would let me play around with his, until he bought me my own." She then started another familiar tune. Billy joined in singing. She was really good. Mark hadn't heard a harmonica since Vietnam. It made him feel strange, very strange. He wondered what else was in store for them as they helped her. She was sending them on a bizarre trip down a not so happy memory lane. There was definitely something about this kid.

The visual evidence on her back was overwhelming proof that she had been in war. But, looks could be deceiving. They'd proven that numerous times over the years. The wound was real, that he was sure of, but the rest of her back and arms could've been a good makeup job. He'd seen Rick pull off some amazing looks over the years.

Then there was the story about how they escaped the POW camp. Could that be something recorded in their military files? The kid that helped them was Vietnamese; Sam's eyes are blue.

There was something about her that made him want to believe her, but the story was just too strange to be true. He couldn't help but thinking that this could be an elaborate hoax by Walters to get them to drop their guard. There was no such thing as a twenty-two year old Marine Corps. General. Were they really supposed to feel safe under "her protection"? No, he had a strange feeling about her.

When they stopped for dinner, Billy went inside with Sam. Rick hung back with Mark for a moment. They were in agreement; they felt torn. Something didn't add up; they agreed they needed to be ready for anything. Unlike Billy, they didn't trust this kid. The problem was that Billy was going to help her, and they weren't about to leave Billy unprotected.

Reno, Nevada

It was dark as they drove into Reno. Sam gave directions how to get to Carter's house. As they got out of the van, two young black girls ran up to them, calling "Sammy!" Sam squatted down and embraced both of them. She spent a few minutes talking with them. They had a lot of things they wanted to tell her. A woman walked up the street and stood a few feet away; she was smiling. Eventually, Sam looked over to her and said. "Hi, Janie, how are you?"

"I'm well. It's good to see you, Sam. They've missed you."

The girls wanted Sam to carry them inside. She told them she had hurt her shoulder, so they would have to be careful. She had the older girl get on her back and hold on around her neck. Sam had the younger girl get on her sister's back. Sam stood up giving both of them a piggy back ride. She turned to the team and told them to follow her.

Once inside, Janie told them Simon had been staying with them, but he had moved out. "Nick knows where he is, but he's at work right now and won't be home until almost 2am."

"I need to find Simon right away. We'll go see him at work."

Mrs. Carter gave Sam the address of the bar where her husband was working. "I know Nick would love to see you. But Sam, it's a rough part of town. Watch your back."

"Thanks for the heads up. We'll be careful."

The two little girls were disappointed they were leaving so soon. They were holding a guitar and wanted Sam to play for them. She agreed to play one song. It took her several minutes to tune the guitar. Mrs. Carter commented. "We only keep it for when you come to visit."

Sam smiled. The two little girls sat at her feet with excited anticipation. Sam asked if they wanted to hear a new one or an old one. They chose a new one. She then began playing a song so beautiful that Mark was immediately captured in its tune and lyrics. The song seemed to end all too soon as the little girls were clapping and telling Sam they liked it. She gave them hugs and told them to be good. She'd see them soon.

They arrived outside of the bar where Carter worked. Mark noticed they were in a very unsavory part of town. As they walked into the bar, that uneasy feeling he got gripped him as he noticed the bar was full of black men all staring at them. A large man walked up to them. "Your kind is not wanted here."

Rick stepped in front of Sam. "And what kind would that be?"

"Whites. You need to leave, now!"

Sam spoke up. "I'm here to see Nick Carter; and I'm not leaving until I do."

Mark knew what was coming next. He hated this part. Fists started flying and they were in a bar fight.

He thought he saw Sam run up the wall and do a flip over a guy. She was holding her own. He wasn't sure how much time passed before he heard the shotgun fire and a man yell. "Sammy stop!"

Chapter 4

When Mark turned around, Sam had the leader on his knees with a knife at his throat. The entire bar was still, staring at her. There was a look in her eyes. The man called out again in a strong, firm voice. "Sammy, let him go."

Sam released her grip and then kicked the guy in the back, knocking him to the floor. "You owe Carter your life." She told him in a deadly, serious tone.

The black man with the shotgun was a slender man, about six feet tall; and was suddenly by her side. They exchanged a fisted type of hand jibe. Carter then said. "Barker, that's enough from you and your guys. We're not going to have any more trouble tonight. Just sit and enjoy your beers." Carter turned to Sam, "You and your friends come with me."

They followed him to a private room in the back of the bar. Once the door closed behind them, Carter gave Sam a huge smile as he picked her up and spun her around. "How are you, kid? It's so great to see you. I heard about what happened. Are you alright?"

"I'm fine." She told him grinning.

"You should be resting. Here, have a seat. All of you, come sit down." Carter motioned them over to a table surrounded by chairs. "Would you like some beers?"

They all said 'yes' and Carter disappeared for a few minutes, returning with beers for everyone except Sam. "Sammy, I brought you a fancy chocolate milk. Give it a try. I've been trying to perfect the recipe. So, what are you doing here?"

"I'm looking for Simon. He hasn't called in. I think he's in trouble. Do you know where he is?"

"Yeah, I don't know where he's living, but I do know where he's working. It's a new job driving trucks for a shipping company. He's been working there a couple of weeks now. It was a bit of a drive from my place, so he got a room closer.

"So, Sam, what do you think of the chocolate milk?"

"It's good, really good."

"Would you like another one?"

"Yeah, sure."

He left the room again and returned a moment later, handing Sam another drink. She drank it down as fast as the first one.

Rick started asking questions about the shipping company. Mark was watching Carter, he was a jubilant, friendly guy.

Sam then caught his attention. "Carter, what did you put in my drink?"

"It's only vodka, Sammy."

"What? Why?"

"You need to rest." His voice was full of concern.

"Carter! I can't focus or think straight."

Carter wrapped his arms around her. "Sammy,

you don't need to. No one is going to be shooting at you or trying to blow you up. You're not in Nam. You're in a safe place. Now, listen to me. I'm your big brother and you almost died two days ago. I'm not going to let you chase after Simon unless you are well rested. So stop fighting the alcohol and just relax."

"Carter." She still tried to protest, but Mark could tell the alcohol was winning.

"I'm taking guard watch tonight, so you have nothing to worry about. I'm not going to let anything happen to you. Sleep, Sammy. I love you, little sister."

"I love you too." She mumbled and then completely passed out.

Carter kissed her on the forehead. He then picked her up into his arms and walked across the room with her. He placed her on a built in bench that ran along one of the walls. Billy offered his jacket to use as a pillow.

Carter then sat at the table with them. "Let's talk."

"We have a few questions." Rick told him. "For starters, if you're good friends, why did you just knock her out?"

"She's exhausted; I can see it in her eyes. Sammy doesn't sleep well; she hasn't for years. I'm hoping the alcohol will help her get a good rest tonight."

"Fair enough. You seemed concerned in the bar. What did you think she was going to do to that guy?"

"I didn't know. Her mind has been a little bit confused lately. You see, Sammy's been fighting the Vietnam War her entire life. Her fighting is instinctive. She could have easily killed him and then when she realized what she had done, she would've taken it really hard. Barker is scum and someone should take him out, but letting Sammy do it isn't worth the nightmares it will cause her. She has enough of those already."

"You'll have to excuse me for having a hard time believing she was in Vietnam. I'll admit I've seen and heard some strange things, but still. This sounds like a tall tale to me."

"I understand your skepticism. If I hadn't lived it myself, I'd have a hard time believing it too. Look, I can prove it." Carter took a picture out of his wallet. It was one of the same pictures Mark had seen at Anthony's house. "We were in the same unit in Nam. Here's me, Simon, Lieutenant Anthony, Sergeant Anderson, Captain Matthews, Paz, Kelly, and that right there is Sammy."

They all looked at the photograph. Mark couldn't believe it, but as he looked closely at the picture, he could recognize her face.

"Sammy was an orphan." Carter continued. "She pretended to be one of the guys and we all covered for her. Anyone else who met her thought she was just a short guy and it helped she hadn't started puberty yet. She could handle a gun, and you wanted to be next to her in a firefight. I can't tell you how many times she saved our lives. Simon called her our guardian angel."

"You said she almost died a couple of days ago. I assume that has to do with the bullet wound in her shoulder?"

"Yeah, you see, the U.S. officially pulled out of

Vietnam four years ago, but Sammy is head of a secret group who goes back into Nam to rescue our POWs left behind. They operate without a safety net."

"Suicide missions." Rick commented. "Something goes wrong, and the U.S. government denies any involvement."

"You got it. There was chatter on the line of an American who was being held prisoner. Sammy and her team went in. Sammy has an in and out maneuver that she's perfected over the years. She reminds me of a cat burglar; they get the POWs on the chopper before the NVA even knows they're missing. They had made it to their rendezvous point in Thailand and gotten on The Beluga, their C-141 Starlifter, to fly to Los Angeles.

"The guy they rescued had been really quiet. They gave him some food, and Sammy had gotten on the horn to start looking for the guy's family. That's something that's very important to her. She makes sure someone is there in L.A. to meet every person they bring home. Sammy had her back to the guy when he suddenly grabbed a gun and opened fire on all of them. She was the first one hit. My and Won finally wrestled the guy down and knocked him out, but not before almost everyone in the unit had been shot. Doc was the only one without injury, because he'd been in the john when the shooting started.

"Sammy immediately starting helping Doc apply pressure dressings on people and administering fluid. She said she was fine, had only been nicked. But they all knew she was worse off. Chang had had a bullet graze his head and was one of the first ones bandaged. He kept a close eye on Sammy, knowing she would fight anyone who tried to stop her from providing medical treatment. Every time he tried to get close, she would order him to go help someone else. They knew she was bleeding to death, but she wouldn't let anyone near her. She was determined to save her unit, first. Eventually, she was too weak to stand. Chang rushed her and had to knock her out to save her. They diverted course, landed, and all went to the hospital. Thankfully, everyone was able to be saved."

"What happened to the guy who fired on them?" Billy asked.

"Doc kept him sedated until they got him to the Naval Hospital at Camp Pendleton."

"You said Sam hadn't been thinking straight lately. Anthony also said something similar." Rick commented. "What exactly do you mean?"

"The Sarge came home a couple of weeks ago and found Sammy on the roof of the house. She was firing her pistol. He climbed up and asked her what she was doing. Sammy told him the NVA were attacking, but not to worry, because she was taking them out one at a time and they weren't going to take their home. It scared him to death; and she's had several hallucinations since then. Also, her nightmares are getting more frequent and intense. She's been fighting for too long. We think she might be going crazy."

"There were guys who lost it only spending a year over there." Mark reflected. "Just look at Billy."

"Do you think Simon's in trouble or is it all in her head?" Rick asked Carter.

“Simon has a knack for getting into trouble. He also loves the ladies and could have forgotten to call. It’s hard to tell. It almost doesn’t matter; Sammy will go non-stop until she finds him. That’s why I knocked her out with the vodka. Sammy doesn’t drink. I want to make sure she’s well rested in case he really is in trouble.

“You see, Simon and Sammy are really close. Simon and I were there the day the Sarge found her in Vietnam. It was 1968. She was twelve-years-old. While the Sarge taught her good moral values, Simon taught her how to lie, scam people, cheat at poker, and so forth. He taught her how to act like one of the guys and helped her blend in. Sammy looks up to him like a big brother. I don’t think Simon could ever do anything wrong in her eyes. I remember this time we were joined with another unit. Some of the guys were upset saying the black man was being treated as a second class citizen, because the white commanding officers gave us jobs like walking point. Simon always gravitated toward trouble, and this was no different. He started hanging out with this guy named Freedman, who was the leader of the protest. One night there was a gathering to play cards, a kind of party. Sammy wanted to go; Simon had always let her go with him. He told her she couldn’t come, because of the color of her skin. She wasn’t black. Sammy protested, but Simon’s temper was short and he yelled at her that she couldn’t come.

“Now, Sammy didn’t understand the racial tension that was building between the black and white soldiers. She saw all of us as Americans. And Simon and her were buddies; he'd never yelled at her before. You see, Sammy was like a chameleon; Vietnamese one minute, American the next. The way she thought, it was no big deal changing the color of her skin. If she needed it to be black, she'd just change it.

"When Simon and I got back from the party, we found her hanging by her wrists in the bunkhouse. Her skin was covered in black mud. She was unconscious and had been beaten badly. We both knew she had tried to go to the party.

"Simon was beside himself. We cut her down, and he carried her to the Sarge's tent, while telling her to hang on and how sorry he was. The Sarge reamed Simon out, but the guilt he felt was a greater punishment. Sammy didn't wake up for three days, and Simon didn't leave her side, nursing her the entire time. When she finally woke up, Sammy confirmed Freedman and a couple of his friends had beaten her. Simon asked her why she hadn't fought back, because we knew she could have taken them. She simply told him, because Freedman was an American and Simon's friend. She didn't want Simon to be angry with her. Simon cried and hugged her, telling her how sorry he was. He also told her that American or not, she was to always defend herself.

"Simon then went mental; and after Freedman. The LT and Sarge had to pull him off before he killed the guy. The LT had Freedman charged with assault on another soldier and had him arrested. Freedman tried to say he was being arrested because he was black, but Simon made sure everyone knew that wasn't it. Since the other two guys were just following

Freedman, Sammy and Simon made special plans for them. They kidnapped them; and Sammy went after them her own special way. The guys were scared so badly that they both crapped themselves. For the remainder of the time they were with us, they would keep their distance from Sammy.

"Simon reupped for a second tour, because he didn't want to leave Sammy behind. And when we finally got papers for Sammy to come to the U.S.; she negotiated for Simon to rotate out to The States to finish his tour as her Sergeant.

"If Simon is in trouble, Sammy will handle it. I'm just worried she's going to forget where she is; and she'll mount a full assault. You can't let her kill anyone; it'll eat her up inside and might push her completely over the edge."

"We'll do our best to get her to let us do the heavy." Rick tried to reassure him.

"I appreciate you helping Sammy." Carter seemed very sincere. "Another thing, if you don't find Simon tomorrow, please let me know. She needs to be with one of us the day after tomorrow. I'll come to wherever you are to stay with her that day."

"The anniversary of her brother's death." Mark remembered.

"Yes. Despite being lethal, Sammy is one of the most caring, loving people you will meet. She blames herself for Paul's death. It wasn't her fault. We were there. It was just a horrible accident. She should be with one of us, so she doesn't have to face the day alone."

"We'll make sure she has the support she

needs." Billy told him.

Carter carried Sam to the van and put her on the back bench. "I'll join you at the hotel as soon as I get off work. If she starts to have a nightmare, please wake her up right away."

Mark and Billy shared an adjoining room with Sam. Mark conned Billy into staying up with her until Carter arrived. As Mark looked over at her one last time before heading into his room, he noticed she looked so peaceful sleeping. Mark thought back on how much he'd learned about her in the past twenty-four hours. It was still hard to believe she was who she said she was. One thing was for sure, she did look like an angel when she slept.

The following morning came all too early. The night had not been restful. Sam had woken up several times with nightmares. Mark vaguely remembered Billy being there for the first one or two, and then Carter for the others.

After eating breakfast, he was off to the shipping company. The team had convinced Sam to stay at the hotel with Billy while they gathered information and looked for Simon. Mark was hoping to find him easily and bring him back to her; assignment over.

It didn't turn out that way. He had read the job roster and found a route Simon was scheduled to take. They had tracked down the truck, but Simon wasn't driving it. They had also found the room Simon was renting, but was told he hadn't been there in several days. They seemed to be hitting one dead end after another. Rick had a hunch, something strange was going on at the shipping company. They decided to visit the owner and run a wiretap. The tap paid off, there was a conversation about Simon. It was time to move in.

Chapter 5

"Rick!" Sam protested when she was told she wasn't coming with them. "Now, I have patiently sat here all morning and half the afternoon like you wanted me to. But can you stand here and tell me that if it were Mark or Billy that you would just sit back and let someone else rescue them? Or would you be helping? You can't tell me that an extra person coming to help, especially one who specializes in search and rescue, wouldn't add value to the mission."

"Alright, kid, you can come, but I'm not giving you a gun; and I'm in charge. We made a promise that we would make sure you didn't kill anyone."

Sam half grinned. "Believe me, I have no intentions of killing anyone. That's murder in this country and the last thing I want to do is spend the rest of my life in jail."

"Alright team, now that we're all in agreement, let's mount up." Rick said the word and they all jumped in the van to head to the owner's house in the country.

Mark looked through the metal, black rods of the fence surrounding the grounds. "Rick, this place is huge. How are we going to find Simon? We don't even know if he's here. I hope you have a plan."

"May I make a suggestion?" Sam spoke up.

"Sure." Rick told her.

"There's a guard there at ten o'clock."

"Where?" None of them could see him.

"Use your binoculars." She suggested.

Rick looked. "Okay, I see him now."

"Why don't we get him to tell us where Simon is? We can get in and out with Simon without anyone knowing we were ever here."

"Interesting." Mark could tell from the look on Rick's face he was mulling over the idea. "But why would the guard just tell us?"

"I'll have him so scared; he'll tell us anything we want to know." Sam said confidently.

Mark would have to be lying if he didn't say he wasn't at least a bit curious about what she would do. He watched the familiar smile come across Rick's face. "Okay. This sounds interesting. Mark, go with her. Billy, make your way to the other side of the property and take the left flank. I will stay with the van to cover you and come in to get you, if you need a quick exit."

"Do you have a ball that will fit into my hand?"

"Yes, I believe so." Billy told her and started looking in the van.

"I'll need some rope too."

Billy found both items and handed them to Sam. She turned to Mark. "I'll need you to carry the rope. I'll take point."

They were off. Mark was amazed at how effortlessly Sam climbed over one of the brick pillars of the fence. He followed her as they crouched and snuck through some trees to move closer to the guard. When they were only a few feet away, she motioned him to stay. Sam then stood up and walked over to the guard. "Hello," she smiled and said. "Grenade." She threw the ball up into the air causing the guard to look up.

The next few seconds happened so fast, Mark wasn't sure exactly what had happened. Sam had the guy on his knees with her arms wrapped around his throat. "Now," she told the guard who was having difficulty breathing. "I'm a trained killer, but I'm going to give you a choice. You can tell me what I want to know and I'll let you live; or my friend here will tie you up and I'll torture you in ways you can't even imagine. You'll be begging for me to kill you when I get done."

Mark interjected. "She's brutal. I wouldn't mess with her, if I were you."

"Okay, Okay." The guard said. "I'll tell you what you want to know."

"Where is Joe Simon?"

"He's being held in the basement."

"If you are lying to me, I'll hunt you down and kill you."

"I'm telling the truth. I swear."

Sam then finished the sleeper move, causing just enough oxygen loss to cause the guy to black out.

"Nighty, Night." Mark grinned. "He'll have one heck of a headache when he wakes up." Mark got on the walkie-talkie to Rick. "We know where Simon is. We're going into the house to get him."

Sam turned to Mark. "What's a basement?"

"It's an area under the house. There will be a door inside the house with stairs that lead to it."

"Like a tunnel?"

"Yes, except it doesn't go anywhere. It's just a room."

"Got it. Let's go." And she was off.

Mark had to move quickly to keep up with her. As he followed her across the yard and through the house, he was impressed with her skills. They eventually found a door that lead to the staircase. Sam cautiously descended. As they cleared the first few steps and started to get a view into the place, Sam suddenly said, "Simon!", while running down the remaining stairs.

He was tied to a chair, had signs of being badly beaten, and was unconscious. Sam tried to wake him with no luck. Mark got on the walkie-talkie, "Rick, we found Simon. He's unconscious. We're bringing him out."

Sam turned to him. "Mark, you're going to have to carry him."

Mark caught Simon as Sam released the ropes. He struggled at first to lift the six-foot-black man over his shoulder. Suddenly, there was gunfire.

"We have to get out of here! Give me your gun. I'll lead us out and cover you."

"Sam, I can't give you my gun."

"There's no time for arguing. We need to get out of here, and I can't carry him with my shoulder shot up."

Mark knew she was right, but he was torn about giving her the gun. She seemed mentally stable to him, but could she suddenly go crazy?

"Please, trust me!"

"Alright," he agreed and handed her the gun.

She led them cautiously up the staircase with the gun drawn and poised to shoot. The hallway was clear, so far so good. They entered a room which looked like a living room. It contained a huge two story window wall.

They heard someone coming. Sam aimed the gun in the direction of the sounds. They continued to slowly move forward. Mark felt his body tense up which made the weight of Simon's body feel that much heavier.

Suddenly, the man was right in front of them. Sam lowered the gun; and Mark sighed in relief.

"Billy, get them out of here. I'll cover the rear." Sam told him.

As they headed out of the room, Mark heard another shot and then a waterfall of glass falling behind him. They made it to the front of the house; Mark could see the van waiting for them. They were almost there. Billy started shooting his machine gun while Mark and he ran for the van. Billy helped him get Simon inside while Rick provided cover. "Where's Sam?"

Mark was startled. "She was right behind us."

A moment later, he saw her come running from inside the house. She was firing the gun as she ran. Once they had her in the van, Rick floored it to get them out of there. They sped down the road.

"Have you lost them?" Sam asked Rick.

"We're good. We shot out their tires."

"Can you find a side road, some out of the way

place to stop the van where they can't find us?

"Why do you want to stop?" Rick inquired.

"There's a car coming to join us. It's my medic. We need to stop the van."

"Okay, there is a road to the left up ahead. Let's see what we can find." Rick then turned back to Sam. "How will they be able to find us?"

"My dog tags aren't usual tags; they are a bit thicker. There is a tracking device, so that my team can find me. They have been following us this entire time from a distance. I've just activated the emergency beacon. They are coming to meet up with us." As she spoke the words, Mark thought her speech seemed strained. However, he was more alarmed to learn they had been tracked and followed for two days.

"You've had us followed!" Rick suddenly said. "Kid, I'm not interested in getting caught in a trap."

"Relax, Major, all I want is my medic. His name is Graham. He's five-foot-ten with light brown hair. He's forty-two years old. Graham is under my command and knows you are all under my protection."

Mark thought she looked like she was shaking. She had wrapped herself up in the blanket Billy had given her the previous day. Before he could speak the words, Billy asked, "Are you alright?"

"I'm fine." She quietly replied. "Please stop the van, so Graham can help Simon."

The team found a secluded place to park. They then left Sam and Simon in the van with Mark keeping guard. Rick and Billy positioned themselves to get the jump on the approaching car.

Mark made Sam move to the front of the van,

away from Simon. He kept a close eye on her, making sure she wasn't going to try anything like the move she did on the guard earlier that afternoon. She sat very still and seemed to be really tired; her eyes kept closing and opening slowly like someone who was falling asleep and trying hard to stay awake.

The car arrived and there were two men inside. One with light brown hair jumped out of the driver's side.

"Hold it right there." Billy told him pointing a machine gun.

The man immediately raised his hands above his head. "My name is Graham. I'm here to see Sam Anderson. I'm responding to a medical emergency."

Billy moved forward to pat him down. "He's clean, Major."

"We don't have any weapons on us." Graham told them.

Rick appeared from the other side. "You were at the diner where we had dinner last night."

"Yes, we were checking on Sam. Please Major Peters, this is an emergency. Where is she?"

"You there in the car, slowly get out and keep your hands up where I can see them."

"That's going to be difficult." Graham told them. "If you remember, Scott was on crutches last night; he will need them to get out of the car."

Billy moved in, while Rick held a gun on the man.

"Okay, you can use your hands to get out of the car, but don't make any sudden moves or I'll drop you."

The other man slowly got out of the car. He was around Rick's age and had a cast of his left leg. Billy patted him down. "He's clean."

"Gentlemen, please understand that we don't trust the military and have to be cautious."

"We understand, but we are here to help." Scott told him.

The team lowered their guns.

"Where's Sam?" Graham asked. "I have to get to her right away."

"She's in the van." Rick told him.

As Graham sprinted over to the van, Mark slid open the door. "She's in the front seat."

Graham grabbed the handle and swung open the door. "Sam, what's the problem?"

"I'm fine, check on Simon." She was barely audible.

He checked her eyes; then he placed his hand on her forehead. "You're not fine. Where are you hit?"

Mark suddenly realized that she looked terrible. Her face was very pale, and she was shaking badly. When had this happened?

"Simon." Sam firmly responded.

"I'm going to check on Simon, and then I'm going to be right back for you."

"I'm counting on it. Check my back."

Graham turned to Mark. "Take her pulse for me. Scott! Get the tarp on the ground! Sam's been hit!"

Mark grabbed her wrist and started counting. He couldn't believe how high it was climbing. "It's 140." He noticed that she had closed her eyes. He checked her forehead, she was burning up with fever.

Graham came back. "Simon's going to be just fine. Sam. Sam." He lifted her over his shoulder and carried her to the tarp. Scott was down on his knees. They flipped Sam into his arms and laid her down.

Graham pulled off the blanket. “Dear God!”

Chapter 6

Mark couldn't believe his eyes. Her entire back looked like a minefield covered in holes. Blood was everywhere. There were shards of glass sticking out of some of the holes. The bullet wound had even been ripped open.

"I don't have enough blood." Graham quietly commented.

"I'll get what you need." Scott told him.

"They won't be able to get it here in time."

"Don't worry about it. Just do your thing."

Graham ripped open Sam's shirt and bra with a knife. Rick offered to help dig out the glass and stitch her up. Mark was asked to do rolling pulse counts. Billy went with Scott to the car and carried equipment over to Graham. He then helped hold bandages to try to slow down the blood loss.

Scott got on a portable radio he had brought. "Zach, we have a code crimson! We need Sam's blood right away; a whole container of it. We need it now!"

"I'm on it. Standby." Responded a man's voice.

Mark watched as everyone worked to try to stop the bleeding. Graham assessed which holes were the worst. Rick and he would tackle those first while Billy and Mark kept pressure on the others. Mark kept counting and calling out her pulse. They had had a lot of practice patching up people in Vietnam, and this reminded him of that experience. He'd seen some horrible things, and this was one of them. Sam was in bad shape and losing a lot of blood at a rapid rate.

It wasn't long before the last bag of blood was being attached to her arm. Her pulse was still rising. Graham was working as fast as he could. "Come on, Sam. You are the toughest kid I've ever met. Fight this."

Scott sat down at the top of her head. "Setup a direct blood transfusion from me to her."

"I won't have enough."

"Graham," He calmly said. "She's the first one off the chopper and the last one back on. She makes sure everyone else receives medical treatment before she does. She's the last one to eat; and she won't rest until we have found someone to meet every POW in Los Angeles, so they have a friendly face to come home to. Sam always puts everyone else first. It's time we put her first. You take as much blood as you need; and you save her life. That's an order, Major."

Graham closed his eyes for a second, took a deep breath, and patted Scott on the arm. "I'm going to need for you to lie completely still. You have to tell me when you start to feel cold. I'm going to be draining your blood at a rapid rate. I'll be asking you questions to help me monitor the flow rate. Be completely honest, so I don't kill you both."

"You got it." Scott replied and then got back on the radio. "What's the status of that plane?"

"We're sourcing the blood now and fueling up the

plane."

"Zach, I'm enacting protocol chain of command. Graham is acting commanding officer."

"What's going on? I know Sam's down, but why aren't you in charge?"

Graham got on the radio. "Scott's blood is what's keeping Sam alive right now. I need that plane, Zach!"

"I understand."

Mark looked at Sam. He barely knew her, but the time they had spent together had been definitely memorable. She had an amazing smile and way with people. He felt like he had finally seen what Billy knew all along. She hadn't lied to them and had even protected them from Col. Walters. Mark felt guilty for those moments he had not trusted her. She was dying, and they had even slowed down her medic from getting to her. Mark knew that every second counted when someone was bleeding to death. The guilt was overwhelming.

He got a cloth, poured water on it, and placed it on her forehead. She was burning up with fever from the infection caused by the glass pushing the fabric of her shirt into her body. Her pulse was still rising, 145. If it hit 150, she was dead. "Come on, kid. Hang in there. We're all trying to save you."

Zach came on the radio. "Max is loaded and ready to go."

"Clear the runway and get that plane off the ground!" You couldn't miss the urgency in Graham's voice.

"I'm starting to feel cold." Scott told him.

"Can I get one of you to take his pulse?"

Billy moved over and read the number. Scott's pulse was climbing.

Graham was back on the radio. "Is Max off the ground yet?"

"No, we have a VIP coming in."

"I don't care if it's The President, get that plane off the ground!"

"Roger that. Stand by."

A few moments passed before Zach was back on the radio. "Max is away; and we just pissed off a congressman."

"ETA?"

"30 minutes."

"We don't have 30 minutes."

"I'm clearing all air traffic in the flight path. Max will have a straight shot to you. I'm patching him into our radio, now."

"Max, we need you here."

"I have the engines at full throttle. I'm going to try to squeeze a little more juice out of this baby. Tell Sam and Scott to hang on."

Scott held his hand out for the radio receiver. "Zach, can you patch me into my house?"

"Sure thing. Patching lines. The phone is ringing."

"Hello." A young lady's voice answered.

"Hey Kali, it's Dad." Scott answered.

"Dad!" She sounded excited. "Mom and I were just talking about our trip to Atlanta tomorrow to look for a wedding dress."

"I want you to get your favorite one. I don't care what it costs."

"Oh my gosh, thank you Dad! I'm so excited! I can't believe I'm getting ready to graduate college and get married. I was thinking about asking Sam to be a bridesmaid. She would have to wear a dress for the first time. Do you think she would do it?"

"Sam would do it for you."

"Okay, I'll ask her when you get back home. By the way, when are you coming home?"

"It shouldn't be much longer, a couple more days."

"I was hoping you could walk me down the aisle in your Marine Corp uniform. Would you mind wearing it?"

"Anything you want." Scott smiled. "Hey listen, I don't have much time left, is your mom around?"

"Yeah, she's right here."

"I love you, Kali."

"I love you too, Dad. Here's mom."

"Hey, is something wrong?" A concerned woman's voice answered. "You never call when you're on a mission."

"No, nothing's wrong. I just wanted to let you know that I told Kali she can have whatever wedding dress she wants tomorrow, regardless of price."

"Scott Russell, what's gotten into you? We have a budget for this wedding."

"Not tomorrow you don't. I want my two favorite ladies to have a great day, on me. Treat yourselves to a nice lunch, get your nails done, and pick out the most beautiful dress for Kali."

"I always knew under that tough exterior you were a softy inside. Thanks, sweetie. We can't wait for you to get home."

"Me neither. I love you, Jen, with all my heart. I'll see you soon. Bye."

"I love you, too. Have a safe trip home. Bye sweetheart."

Zach's voice was back on the radio. "The line is clear."

"I want them to have a good day tomorrow." Scott said into the radio. "Can you guys do that for me? Graham, will you walk Kali down the aisle?"

"I'm planning on you walking your own daughter down the aisle...Yes, I'll take good care of them."

"Thanks...I'm really cold."

"I know. You're going to start fading in and out soon. It's time to keep you talking."

"Sam is the same age as Kali." Scott commented. "Over the years, it's been a strange contrast to see their lives. Kali grew up as a typical American kid, going to school and having normal kid challenges. Sam never really got to be a kid. She was fighting a war and leading rescue missions into enemy territory. She didn't get to go to school; had to learn it when she could. When we were all sleeping after a mission, Sam would be in the cockpit with Max having an algebra class. She never once complained about having to be home schooled and squeeze school work in on top of everything else."

"She never complains about anything." Graham commented. "She just takes what life gives her and accepts it. She has the biggest heart of anyone I've ever met. Sam's an amazing kid."

"How's she doing?"

"We've about got all the bleeding to stop, but I'm having difficulty getting her to stabilize. She's really weak."

"And me?"

"You're destabilizing and starting to become critical. I need for you to keep talking and stay awake. Max really needs to get here."

The sun was setting, so Rick set up some lights around the tarp. Mark and Billy were still calling out Sam and Scott's pulses.

"I remember the first time I saw Sam." Scott continued. "They had told us she was twenty-five. I thought to myself 'that's the shortest twenty-five year old I've ever seen.'"

Graham laughed. "I thought the same thing."

"One of the first things she did was remove all of our ranks. She was the Captain, Chang the First Lieutenant, Simon was the Sergeant, and everyone else was Corporals. If you didn't like it, leave."

"A lot of guys left that first five minutes. All of us were officers."

"She was right." Scott reflectively commented. "There was no place for egos or rank with what we were doing. Sam's very particular with who she works with. That first two months of training was intense. Sam had to not only weed us out, but erase our way of thinking and get us to think like her."

"I don't think I slept at all." Graham added. "You never knew when you were going to be kidnapped by the Lihn Ma and strung up by your ankles. I think it happened to me every night for the first two weeks."

Scott laughed and nodded his head in

agreement.

"Hang on a second." Mark interrupted. "The Lihn Ma was an urban, Vietnamese legend of ghosts who slit the NVA soldier's throats and rescued the American POWs. We heard about it when we were prisoners. Are you saying they really exist?"

"The ghosts are real." Graham told them.

"I'll never forget our first mission." Scott continued. "I remember telling Sam to let us go with them. She turned to me and said, 'No, you're not Vietnamese; we are. You'll get captured; we won't.' We had to hide and watch as those kids snuck onto an NVA base, stole critical enemy intel, and pulled out six POWs."

"I can't believe we took a thirteen-year-old, twelve-year-old, ten-year-old, and nine-year-old into combat with us. And by Sam's rules, they were in charge."

"Sam always said the enemy wouldn't be suspicious of orphaned kids." Scott's speech was starting to slur. His eyes were opening and closing. "She was right. They never suspected the kids were trained combat soldiers. I hated having to sit back and watch them get treated as punching bags at times, especially My. She was so tiny. I remember the time Sam got captured and we had to sit and watch her get beaten, because Chang wouldn't let us move in until nightfall. I still don't know how she escaped."

"Scott, you just reminded me of something. Isn't there a story about Sam being captured, escaping, and Simon giving her blood?"

There was silence. Mark had just been listening

to their stories, intrigued to learn more about Sam. Now, he looked over and saw Scott's eyes were closed. He listened to the pulse reading given by Billy; 146. Scott needed blood soon or he was going to die.

Graham was on the radio. "Zach, what blood type is Simon?"

There was a pause and then, "You just found some A positive."

"Can you guys move Simon out here?" Graham was suddenly moving quickly. He stopped the blood flow from Scott to Sam; and started pulling out more transfusion tubes. Rick grabbed Simon and laid him down beside Sam. Graham inserted the needle and started flowing the blood.

"What's the plan, Doc?" Rick asked.

"Sam's not stable yet, but she's close. If I can use Simon's blood to finish giving her what she needs, it will stop Scott's blood loss. He's not stable, but it might just buy us enough time for Max to get here. Simon isn't critical and can give up a couple of pints. If he were awake, he would be doing the same thing Scott's doing."

"Graham, it's Max." A voice came over the radio. "I have you locked in my sites. I'll be there in about five minutes. I'm going to drop the blood right on top of your head. I'll be coming in hot, so on my mark, cover your ears."

"Roger that. Thank God you're here." Mark saw Graham give off a sigh of relief.

"Here we go." Said the voice on the radio. "On my mark, five, four, three, two, one, ears."

Mark covered his ears as the earth shattering

sound of a jet plane broke the silence. The plane must have been only a few hundred feet off the ground. It was one of the loudest things Mark had ever heard.

The container of blood landed only a few feet away. Rick ran over to retrieve it.

"What the hell was that?" Asked an unfamiliar voice.

Chapter 7

"Simon, be still. You're giving a blood transfusion, and I need to wrap your ribs." Graham told him.

Simon started looking around. He turned his head to the side. "Sammy! What's wrong with her? Is she going to be alright? Graham, what's going on?"

"She saved you, and now you're helping save her."

Simon reached over and took hold of Sam's hand. "You take what blood you need. Save my guardian angel." There was a pause before he continued. "The entire time they were beating me, I knew Sammy would come. She would find me and rescue me. I could see her in my head. I could hear her voice. I remembered what she told me about how to withstand pain when being tortured; I did exactly what she told me. Anytime they would ask me a question, I would answer them in Vietnamese." He chuckled and then winced in pain. "They had no idea what I was saying. Which was too bad, because I was warning them that my Sammy would come. How is she, Graham?"

"She came close to bleeding to death. I've been

having difficulty stabilized her. I just need her to keep fighting a bit longer. I'm worried her mind is elsewhere."

"What day is it?"

"The anniversary is tomorrow."

"Sammy, it's your big brother, Simon. I need for you to stay with me. I'd be lost without you."

"Graham, It's Zach." They heard over the radio. "We'd like a status report."

"I'm trying to stabilize both of them. Max, you got here just in time. Another five minutes and we would have lost Scott."

"We're going to need to make plans for tomorrow." Simon told Graham.

"Given her present condition, I expect her to sleep the entire day. She's very weak. I've been doing a lot of research on how to help Sam. You need to realize that given her age and what happened, she's never going to get over it. Now, that doesn't mean she can't get through it. We need to be there for her, support her, let her do whatever she needs to do to release what she keeps bottled up inside."

"Does Jack know what's going on?" Simon asked.

"No. She was almost gone when I arrived."

Simon reached for the radio receiver. "Zach, it's Simon. Please patch me through to the farm."

A girl picked up on the line. Simon said "Hello" in Vietnamese to her. A man then got on the line. "Simon, where've you been? Sam's looking for you."

"She found me and saved my life, again."

"Is she still with you? Let me speak to her."

Simon and Graham told him what happened. Simon then said, "I'm not going to leave her side. I'm going to bring her home, Sarge."

"You do that. Have her call me when she wakes up."

"Will do."

It took a while longer for Graham to finish the blood transfusions. In between checking on Sam and Scott, he wrapped Simon's busted ribs and examined him for any other serious injuries. Simon's face was beaten and bruised. He was sporting a broken nose, but besides that, he was alright.

Graham got Sam, and eventually Scott, to stabilize. He told them he wanted to make sure they were completely stable before transporting them. They were going to be there for a while longer, and he didn't want to take them far. Graham got on the radio, "Zach, can you book us into the closest hotel to our location? We're going to need four rooms, each with two beds. One set of rooms must be connected, so I can keep an eye on my three patients."

"Do you want us to come and help?"

Graham looked at Rick. "Are you guys going to be around tomorrow, or do you need to take off?"

"We'll stay and help." Rick reassured him.

"Zach, I'm good."

"Since we're going to be helping tomorrow, I think it would be good to know what happened with her brother." Rick said. "We want to be prepared."

"To really understand what happened, I need to give you some background of the events that led up to Paul's death." Simon told him.

With everything that had happened the past two days, Mark was very intrigued to find out more about Sam. He listened intensely to every word Simon said.

1956-1968, Vietnam

"Sammy was born in Quang Ngai Province, in the village of Son Tay, South Vietnam. Her mom was an American missionary from Georgia; her dad was Vietnamese. When Sammy was six, her dad started teaching her how to fight, training her to be a soldier. This was the same year Paul was born.

"Fast forward, Paul was now four; Sammy was ten. Sammy's dad had started beating Sammy and her mother. One day, he started hitting Paul. Sammy jumped in to stop him. He beat her and then beat Paul.

"Sammy was afraid Paul was going to be treated the same way she was, and she wasn't going to let it happen. You see, Sammy knew there was something not right with Paul. He was born deaf, but there was more than that; he didn't act like the other children in the village.

"Now, Sammy's military training had been getting more and more intense. She started using what she learned to protect Paul. When she would be allowed time to play with her friends, she taught them how to fight. The kids also started digging tunnels that only they knew about. Think about when you were a kid and you had a secret clubhouse or hideout. That's what the kids made. They built rooms and started fortifying it with supplies.

"The beatings on Paul were getting worse, so

one day Sammy decided it was enough. She took Paul to the secret hideout for him to live there permanently. The kids agreed to help. They had created their own form of sign language to communicate with Paul. They took turns taking care of him and playing with him. Sammy would always come at night. They would curl up together to sleep like they had done in their hut.

"Sammy told her dad that Paul was dead. For a while, he believed her. Then one day, Paul walked into the village looking for Sammy. He was spotted by their father. Sammy ran to him, put him on her back, and took off into the jungle with him. Their father tried to follow, but he'd trained Sammy well and couldn't.

"That night, the torture began. He tortured her every way you can imagine. He broke bones, he burned her, he cut her, he whipped her; he even shot her. Sammy was determined not to break. She knew that if he broke her, Paul would be dead. She also knew that if she ran, he would take out his rage on her mother, so she stayed and endured.

"His failure to break her, frustrated him. One day, he came up with a new plan. He wrapped a rope around her making it so she couldn't move her arms or legs. The bastard then put her in a box and filled the box with sand. He taped a tube to her mouth and another one to her nose. He then buried her alive.

"He kept her down throughout the night. It terrified Sammy, but it didn't break her. It did, however, cause her hatred for him to grow.

"The following year was filled with more training and more torture. Sammy was taken to Hanoi and presented to Ho Chi Minh as a child soldier. The NVA devised a new war strategy; a kid's army. Sammy went through several months of intense training. The plan was to train an army of children to attack the American troops. It was the NVA's secret weapon against us. Due to Sammy's ability to withstand torture and her keen fighting abilities, they made her commander of the army, a little general.

"Sammy used to say that going to Hanoi was the only time she felt happy. It wasn't what she was doing, but if she were in Hanoi with her father, her mom and Paul could be together; and they were safe.

"When she was home, she taught Chang everything she knew. He would follow her and her dad to the Ho Chi Minh trail; and then head back home to reunite Paul with his mom. Chang would also follow them when her dad would take her and bury her. He knew exactly how to find her. Keyla would make a very thin rice broth, and they would pour it down the tube to feed her.

"The day finally came when the NVA arrived in Quang Ngai. Sammy was twelve. She and her dad were to join them and start the assault against us, The Americans. The night before they arrived, Sammy had a moment to tell her mom what was going on. She told her where Paul was hiding and said she'd be back for both of them. She told her mom that Keyla's family had gone to My Lai to visit cousins and taken Paul with them. Sammy's mom showed her a movie tape she had secretly made, told Sammy that she was an American, and told her to get the tape to us.

"The following morning, the NVA invaded the village. Sammy had been all around the war, but hadn't seen it firsthand. She was unprepared for what actually happened. She said she would never forget. She saw her neighbors and friends attacked. Some were shot and killed, others tortured. They were screaming in terror. Homes were destroyed, burning. There was nothing she could do to stop it. She stayed with her mom and watched out the window in horror.

"Her dad came into the hut, told Sammy it was time to go. Sammy turned to her mom and hugged her 'good-bye'. She then asked her dad if the NVA would leave her mom alone. Her dad told her she wouldn't have to worry about it. He raised a gun and shot her mom right in front of her. Sammy rushed to her mom. The last words she heard was 'get the tape, help the Americans. I love you.'

"Sammy's dad grabbed her and pulled her out of the hut. He told her it was time to leave. Sammy grabbed his gun and shot him point blank, killing him. She then looked around at all the chaos, and took off running. She grabbed the hidden tape and movie camera, and headed into the jungle.

"Her dad had a small plane he kept hidden. Sammy had watched him fly it. She pushed the plane out, started the engines, and got it off the ground. She put tape into the movie camera and started filming. She flew over her village capturing what was happening. The NVA started shooting at her, so she turned the plane and headed south.

"We were out on patrol when we heard a loud crash in the jungle. The Sarge had our unit move in to investigate. We were surprised to find a small plane. The Sarge had me come with him to check it out. We had our guns drawn. When we looked into the cockpit, we saw the biggest blue eyes looking up at us. "Don't shoot, I'm an American." She told us in broken English with her hands up. She had blood running down her forehead from smacking it on the instrument panel when she crashed.

"I looked at the Sarge; he had the most baffled look on his face.

"Sammy slowly reached over and handed him the tape and movie camera. She then handed him her knife. She told him her name was Samay Quach. We later found out her real last name was Tran, but it you called her by her father's name; she'd put a knife to your throat.

"The Sarge had her get out of the plane and called the Doc over to take a look at her head. We then started walking back to the base. The Sarge had me keep a gun on her. I kept her just a couple of feet in front of me. I didn't know what to think. We were about half way back to Gloria when she collapsed. I carried her over my shoulder the remainder of the way. I remember thinking she was so tiny and light.

"The Sarge had Carter and me keep her guarded while he took the tape to Captain Matthews. The tape showed footage of Sammy when she was about seven years old. She spoke her name into the camera in English and then went off to play with her friends. It showed her stealing some food off a table and bringing it to a group of kids hiding under another table. The video showed various clips of Sammy with her mom narrating, saying that Sammy was NVA trained and could give us their secrets. Her mom then begged for us to find Sammy's grandparents and get her to them. The next footage was what Sammy filmed of her village being destroyed.

"Captain Matthews had a big dilemma on his hands. Sammy's tattoo on her left shoulder said she was an NVA general." Simon reached over and rubbed the tattoo on her shoulder. Mark also noticed a tattoo on her other shoulder. It read 'POW MIA You are not forgotten' Simon continued. "However, they had a tape from her mom, who was obviously not Vietnamese. They decided to interrogate Sammy when she regained consciousness. Carter and I kept our guns on her the entire time.

"Sammy asked to see a map and proceeded to tell Captain Matthews the NVA's plans for attack. She told him she wanted to help. Next, she asked for a bucket of water or a sink and some soap; requesting we indulge her for a moment. Carter got a bucket. It was the strangest thing; she started washing her hair. The Sarge handed her a towel to dry it. The shocker came when she was done; we could see that it had turned from black to blonde.

"The next few days, we kept her locked up as a prisoner. We didn't know if we could trust her or not. Sammy would sing American lullabies her mother used to sing to her when she was little. Other than that, her English was very limited. The Sarge would go and talk to her in Vietnamese. Since he was on his third tour, he was fluent; and Matthews trusted his instincts. We then had to go back out on patrol; the Sarge wanted to take her with us as a test. She went with no weapons.

"Sammy spotted a trip line Carter was about to hit

and saved his life. Sammy's intel also proved to be correct and helped us catch Charlie off guard. Needless to say, over the next several weeks a trust developed between the Sarge, Captain Matthews, and Sammy. The Sarge was in charge of her. They spent a lot of time together, and became good buddies." Simon smiled.

"Our lieutenant had been killed, so Lieutenant Anthony rotated in. Anthony was green, fresh out of officer's school. We were out on patrol one day and he ordered us up a hill. Sammy started freaking out, telling the Sarge it was a bad idea.

Chapter 8

"The LT wasn't going to hear it; he was in charge and wanted us to follow his orders. We ended up getting completely pinned down by Charlie. Guys were dying; we were in a mess.

"Sammy went to the Sarge with a plan. The LT agreed to try it. Sammy gave each of us a number. The plan was to slowly stop firing like we had been killed and sneak on our bellies down the mountain while Sammy provided cover. She told the Sarge not to come looking for her.

"I'll never forget the moment she suddenly called out in Vietnamese 'Don't shoot, I surrender.' She was taken as a prisoner. We all knew she had sacrificed herself to save us. We were silent as we made our way back to base. I'll never forget the feeling I had that day.

"We wanted to go looking for her, but were told we weren't going out. The afternoon of the third day, Kelly saw a gook walking toward the perimeter. He alerted me; and I called out for them to stop. The person just kept walking. I pulled out my binoculars and looked. It was Sammy with a beaten face. I called out for no one to shoot; and sent Kelly to get the Sarge.

"Sammy looked like the walking dead. She didn't

respond to me talking to her; her eyes were dazed. She just kept walking forward like she was on autopilot. The Sarge got right in front of her and started talking to her. Her eyes shifted to look directly at him. They then rolled back into her head as she passed out. The Sarge caught her in his arms and realized her back was covered in blood. She had been strung up by her wrists and beaten with a whip. She had lost a lot of blood; and was about to bleed to death.

"The Sarge, LT, and I all donated blood to help save her. After that, the LT listened to her and valued her opinion.

"It had been over three months since Sammy arrived. She had become a valuable member of the unit. But, she was anxious to get back home to check on Paul. Sammy convinced Captain Matthews to take the unit to check on him. In return, she told him she would be able to get intel on Charlie's movements. Captain Matthews had a chopper fly us into Quang Ngai Province with food supplies. We were given one week to meet back at the rendezvous point.

"When we got close to Sammy's village, she made us get down and hide. We were on the edge of the jungle and looking out toward an empty field. On the other side were some damaged huts. The place looked abandoned. However, Sammy had a strange vibe. She made the Sarge and LT promise we wouldn't move no matter what we saw. The Sarge didn't like it, but agreed.

"Sammy took off her Army clothes and underneath she was wearing normal Vietnamese clothes. She got up and walked into the open field.

When she was about half way across, she was told to halt and put her hands above her head. A boy about her size appeared with a machine gun pointed at her. He walked over and tied her hands. He then made her walk towards the huts. Suddenly, two NVA soldiers appeared from behind one of the huts.

"The boy took Sammy to the soldiers. One of them punched her in the stomach with the stock of his machine gun. The boy moved away and behind the soldiers. The next thing I knew, Sammy and the boy had ropes around the soldiers' necks and strangled them to death. The boy and Sammy then exchanged a big bear hug. From out of nowhere, children came running over to them; they were all hugging each other. There was a little boy with blonde hair who Sammy picked up and kissed. I knew, she had found her family.

"We were told to come over and were introduced to Keyla, Chang, (the boy we had been watching), Won, My, Paul, and Annie. We found out that the other children were all siblings. They had been taking care of Paul for her. Keyla was twelve like Sammy. Chang was eleven. Won was nine. My was eight. Paul and Annie were six. Their parents had been killed in a massacre. Paul had made them late meeting up with their parents. They hid in the jungle when Chang realized something was wrong in the village. Chang had watched, but made all the other children hide their eyes. He witnessed the U.S. Army slaughter his parents and cousins.

"The kids had taken on adult roles. Keyla was the mom, cooking the food and taking care of the little ones, Paul and Annie. Chang was the dad; defending the family, teaching Won and My how to fight, and taking them to scavenge for food.

"We were taken to Sammy's secret hideout which was an elaborate network of tunnels and rooms. There were electrical lights strung throughout it. There was even an NVA radio that the kids used to monitor Charlie's activity above the ground. It was impressive how kitted out the place was.

"The kids were wary of us. Chang looked like he was going to murder us at any moment. He hated us, because we were Americans. The kid scared me to death. But Sammy kept him in line and wanted us to all get to know each other and get along.

"I had fun playing with the little kids; Paul and Annie. Paul immediately warmed up to us, he wasn't afraid. Annie quickly followed." Simon gave a little laugh. "I don't know how many horsey rides I gave them. Sammy would sing songs and tell stories. It's the happiest I've ever seen her.

"We all noticed something was off with Paul. The Sarge had grown up in an orphanage and told us there was a kid there that was autistic. Paul reminded him of that kid."

"The day before we were supposed to leave, we were outside. I don't remember what we were doing, but I'll never forget Keyla suddenly screamed. I saw Sammy take off, sprinting across the field. I looked to see what she could be running towards; Paul was getting close to the jungle's edge. He was laughing. When he saw Sammy, he turned to run away from her. It looked like he thought she was playing a game, but she wasn't. Sammy had set up trip wires all along the perimeter. She was almost to him when he hit the line. Sammy was blown backwards. We all thought she was dead. The Sarge and LT took off running toward her. Chang held back Keyla, who was screaming and crying.

"I remember looking at Sammy and realizing that she was moving. She started crawling on her belly toward Paul. When she got to him, she pulled him up into her arms. He was dead, had been killed instantly. She just held him and wouldn't let go. You can still see the shrapnel scars on her arms." Simon rubbed his hand down her left arm. Mark could see them. "There are also some just inside her hairline.

"Eventually, the Sarge was able to get her to give Paul to him. He and the LT wrapped the body in some cloth. I helped dig the grave we buried him in. Sammy didn't speak to anyone, she didn't cry; she just had this hollow, blank stare on her face. I'm convinced part of her died that day.

"The following morning when we woke up, we discovered she was gone along with Chang, Won, and My. Keyla told us not to leave the base; Charlie was nearby. None of us liked it, but we stayed to protect the two girls.

"Around mid-morning Sammy returned with two American POWs they had rescued. The kid's clothes were covered in blood; there wasn't a scratch on any of them. Sammy just simply said, 'Charlie is no longer a threat.' The Sarge found out that the kids had left right after we'd fallen asleep. They'd taken out an entire NVA platoon by slitting their throats. The legend of the Lihn Ma was born.

"It was time for us to meet the chopper. Sammy said 'goodbye' to the kids and told them one day she would come back for them. We all felt terrible having to leave them behind, but the LT said there would be no way we would be able to keep six kids on the base. They would be sent to an orphanage and there was no telling what could happen after that. He reckoned they were safer staying in Sammy's secret base.

"A couple of weeks after we returned to Firebase Gloria, Captain Matthews was killed. The LT and Sarge decided we had to make Sammy one of the guys to keep her with us. The upper command wasn't going to let us keep a kid on the base and with Sammy being a former NVA general, we ran the risk of her being taken prisoner and possibly killed. The Sarge removed his name from one of his shirts and sewed it onto one for Sammy. He also gave her a military haircut. There were a small number of us who knew the truth; we were told to keep her true identity a secret. We all did."

1979 Outside Reno, Nevada

Simon leaned over and gave Sam a kiss on the cheek. "She was our guardian angel." He looked at Graham. "How's she doing, Doc?"

"She's stable. They both are. We can try to

move them to the hotel, but we need to move them slowly and carefully."

"You look like hell." Simon commented. "Are you alright, Graham?"

"I've just watched two of my best friends almost bleed to death." He quietly answered.

"You did an amazing job saving their lives." Rick told him.

"Thank you, sir. I couldn't have done it without all of your help."

They loaded Scott, Sam, and Simon into the van. Graham went with them. Billy and Mark followed in the car. The entire ride, Mark's mind was distant. He was thinking about the stories he had heard about Sam; and what he witnessed her friends were willing to do for her. Now that he knew the truth, he admired and respected her for the sacrifices she had made to save Americans. And the kicker was, he was one of them. That had been hard to wrap his mind around at first, but now it was very clear.

The following morning, the team had breakfast in the hotel lobby. They talked about what had happened the previous night and were all in agreement they would stay and help as long as needed. This mission wasn't over.

Graham had decided to stay up all night to make sure Sam and Scott remained stable. The team headed to his room to take over, so he could get some much needed sleep. They knocked on the door. There was no answer. That was odd.

Mark picked the lock and opened the door. They found Graham on the floor, knocked out. Simon and

Sam were missing. Scott was still unconscious on his bed in the next room.

It took a few minutes to wake Graham up. Once they did, he told them he was in the adjoining room when he heard Simon arguing with someone, so he came to find out what was going on. There were four, black men with guns. Simon was begging them to leave Sam alone. When they picked her up and started to leave with her, Graham tried to stop them and had been clocked on the back of the head. He thought he heard Simon call one of the guys 'Barker', but that was all he knew.

"Barker?" Mark commented. "Wasn't that the name of the guy Sam pulled a knife on in the bar?"

"I think you're right." Rick replied.

They gave Graham ice for his head and helped him to his feet. He was dizzy and had to sit on the bed for a moment. "Sam is still unconscious. She's incredibly weak and shouldn't be moved. She could destabilize. The radio is under Scott's bed. We need to get on the horn to Zach; he can track her."

Mark grabbed the radio and brought it to Graham. "Zach, Sam and Simon have been taken. I need you to run a trace."

"We're here. Hang on a moment. I'll be right there."

There was a knock at the door. Billy let two guys around Mark's age, their early thirties, into the room. One of them rushed over to Graham. He was about 6'2" with jet, black hair. "Are you okay?" He started examining Graham's head.

"I think I have a concussion."

The other guy came in with some military boxes hanging from his shoulders. He started setting up electronic equipment. He was a couple of inches shorter with black hair as well. They both had military buzz cuts. "I'll have the system up momentarily."

"Did you guys drive all night?" Graham inquired.

"No," The guy examining his head responded. "We brought Jolly."

"You brought our Jolly?"

"Yes."

"Max, don't you think flying around in an NVA chopper might cause suspicion?"

"Nope, we covered up the stars." He smiled. "Zach, have you found her yet?"

"I'm locking onto her now. She's on the move."

"Let's go get her."

"Hang on, Max." Graham told him. "I want to get Sam back as much as you do. But, we're not on an official mission, and we're not in Vietnam, where there are no rules. We are U.S. Marines. We can't just go in there attacking civilians with a military helicopter."

"You can't, but we can." Rick told him. "Billy, Mark, and I will go in the chopper. Graham, I think it would be best to move you and Scott to our room, just in case they come back."

"I'll run command from the chopper."

"Zach, you're wounded." Graham commented. "You need to stay here."

"But, this is Sam we're talking about. She goes out on missions with a bullet wound; why can't I?"

"Because I can't stop her." Graham told him.

"He's right, man." Max commented. "Run

command from here; and take care of Graham and Scott. They need you. We'll get her back."

Zach conceded.

"Max, I want you in your helmet and vest." Graham told him. "There's been enough bloodshed this week."

"You got it."

As they climbed aboard the helicopter, Billy commented. "This is no ordinary Jolly Green Giant."

"Nope." Max smiled. "It's a Super Jolly. Sam, Zach, and I designed some of the special features it has. It's a prototype; only one in the world."

"Sam's a pretty unique kid, isn't she?"

"She's one-of-a-kind, that's for sure. If they hurt her, there will be hell to pay." Max commented as he lifted the helicopter off the ground.

It didn't take long for them to track Sam's signal to a truck moving down the highway. Max positioned the helicopter in front of the truck, causing it to stop. Rick, Mark, and Billy jumped out with machine guns.

Mark was surprised to see Simon climb out of the driver's seat.

"Where's Sam?" Max asked him.

"Barker has her. He seems to have some personal vendetta against her. I don't know why. He's going to kill her if I don't run this shipment. You guys have to save her. She's still unconscious." Simon then became overwhelmed with emotion. "I can't believe I got her into this mess."

"What is in this shipment you're running?" Rick inquired.

"It's drugs. When I found out they weren't a legitimate shipping company, but part of a drug smuggling ring; I didn't want anything to do with it. I told them I quit. That's when they beat me up, and Sammy rescued me."

"Simon, check your pockets." Max told him with a look of concern on his face.

Simon reached in and pulled out Sam's dog tags. "How did these get on me?"

"She must have slipped them on you at some point when you were being rescued. She wanted to make sure we helped you. Unfortunately, now we have no idea where she is." Max rubbed his hand on his face in obvious frustration and concern.

"Simon, do you have any idea where she might be?" Rick asked.

"They took us to the house out in the country. It's the same house where they were holding me."

"Alright guys, that gives us an advantage. Mark has already been in the house and knows where Simon was kept. There's a good chance Sam is being held in the same place. We just have to get back into the house and find her. Once she's been rescued, we're going to put an end to Barker's drug smuggling days once and for all." Rick then came up with a plan. They would use the helicopter as a distraction to pull everyone out of the house. Mark would sneak inside and grab Sam. He would then head out the other side of the house and up the road where Graham's car would be waiting. Mark would get Sam into the car and take her to Lt. Anthony's house. Once they were clear, the helicopter would go back and join Simon. They would then get to the root of who was in charge of the smuggling ring and take down the entire organization.

It didn't take long to put the plan into motion. Mark made it into the house and down into the basement. He found Sam lying on the floor. It bothered him to see her just tossed down like she was. He called Rick on the walkie-talkie. "I've found her."

Pulling her up into his arms, Mark slipped her dog tags over her head and tried to wake her. She started to stir and opened her eyes. "Hey, do you think you can walk?" He asked as he heard gun fire starting in the distance.

"I won't be able to move fast enough." She quietly told him, "but if you put me on your back and hand me your gun; I can cover us."

It was an interesting idea. Mark picked her up piggy back style, holding onto her legs. Sam held her left arm around his neck and pointed the gun in aim position with her right hand. Mark headed up the stairs, cautiously opened the door. The hallway was clear, so he quickly moved to the back of the house. Once outside, it was going to be a sprint across the lawn. He took a deep breath and looked around.

"We're clear." Sam whispered into his ear.

Mark took off running. He made it to the fence line and climbed the wooden slats. He stopped for a moment to catch his breath on the other side. Sam climbed off his back and peered through the slats back toward the house. "I don't see anyone following us." She told him.

"Good." He told her still breathing hard. "Get on my back and let's get to the car. It's not much further up the road."

They were off again. Mark's lungs felt like they were straining to get enough oxygen as he ran. Maybe Rick was right; he wasn't in the best shape. Mark was relieved to turn the corner and find the waiting car. He pulled out the walkie-talkie. "We've made it to the car. We're clear."

Mark pulled the keys out of his pocket and opened the passenger side door. He helped Sam off his back and into the car. He then ran around to the other side and put the key into the ignition. The car wouldn't crank. He tried a second time, a third, a fourth. He pulled out the walkie-talkie again. "Rick, we have a problem. The car won't start." There was silence on the other end. "Rick?" No answer.

Chapter 9

"Well, it looks like they're out of range, and we're walking. The nearest town is five or six miles up the road."

"Let's do it." She told him opening the door to get out.

Mark knew she was weak, so he hurried back around to help her. He put his arm around her waist while she placed her arm around his neck. Mark knew they would be sitting ducks if they walked along the road, so he headed into the woods.

They had walked about a mile when Sam said, "Mark, I need to take a break."

"No problem." He gently laid her down on the golden little wildflowers scattered along the ground. "Are you okay on your back?"

"It's alright. Thanks." She had her head turned, looking to the side. "What are those little things flying?"

He turned to where she was looking. He was puzzled by her question. "Those are butterflies. Have you never seen butterflies before?"

"I think I have, but haven't really looked at them closely. I never knew the English word for them. They're peaceful and beautiful."

"Not as beautiful as you are." He suddenly said

looking at the sun dancing off her blonde hair. "But, I'm sure you've been told that many times by guys you've dated."

"No one's ever said that to me." She told him while still watching the butterflies. "I've only been on one date. It didn't go well."

"What happened? If you don't mind me asking."

"My sister, Keyla, asked me to go on a double date with her and her boyfriend." She casually told him. "The guy was friendly, polite, but he had a lot of questions, like why didn't I go to school and how did Keyla and I become sisters. I couldn't answer his questions, 'sorry that's classified information.' It was very awkward. I had to lie to him or switch the subject. But switching subjects didn't work well either, because I couldn't relate to what they were talking about. Then, if things weren't bad enough, we were asked to go swimming. I can't wear a swimsuit in front of people who don't know the truth; not with all the scars on my body.

"Even if my identity wasn't classified, no one would believe I was telling the truth. You didn't believe me when you found out."

"Well...I..."

She smiled. "The reality is, my age doesn't match up to being a vet; I'm ten years too young. My gender doesn't match either; the U.S. Military doesn't allow women to be in combat. Anyone I tried to tell the truth to would think I was lying to them; that I was crazy. I wouldn't want to be in a relationship based on lies. I would want to be myself and be accepted for who I am.

"Nine years ago, I sold myself to the government as a military asset to save the people I love. I don't regret it, and if I was asked today, I would do it again. I made peace with my reality years ago; that I would never have a first kiss, a boyfriend, or anything else that a normal life has. What about you? Do you have a girlfriend?"

"Me? No. I've had lots of relationships, but I can't be in a real relationship while always looking over my shoulder for Walters. I can't tell people who I really am, so I tell lots of lies. I also have to move around a lot to keep from being caught. But one day, I hope to have my name cleared. I'd like to settle down with a woman that I can be completely honest with, maybe have some kids. I hope that one day I can live a normal life."

"I hope you get what you're looking for. It sounds nice."

"Thanks." He sincerely replied. He looked at her, and couldn't get over how stunningly beautiful she was. "I hope I'm not being too forward here, but I would be honored to give you your first kiss."

Sam gave him a surprised look. "You would do that for me?"

"Yes, but only if you would like for me to."

She was silent for a moment, looking at him. "Yes."

Mark leaned in. He wanted to make sure the kiss was special. He caressed her cheek and then gently touched his lips to hers, tenderly kissing her for a few moments and then pulling away to look into her deep blue eyes. She put her hand behind his head and pulled him in for another kiss. This one was deeper, more intense. Mark wanted to kiss her; he enjoyed it immensely. He could tell Sam was enjoying it too. They kissed for a long time, soaking up the moment and each other.

Since Mark was holding himself up, not wanting to put any pressure on her injured back, his arm eventually fatigued causing him to regrettably pull away. He smiled at her.

Sam was smiling back. "Thank you. That was amazing."

"Any time. You're an incredible woman, Sam Anderson." Mark was happy she enjoyed the kiss. It made him feel good to be able to give her something special.

They decided to keep moving. They made it about another mile when she suddenly said, "Mark, I'm sorry, but I have to rest."

"You don't need to apologize. I don't mind." He told her as he helped her down to the ground.

Her eyes had closed. She was too weak to continue. He leaned over and tenderly kissed her on the cheek. Mark then picked her up over his shoulder to start carrying her.

It was a long three mile walk. It reminded Mark of when he was in the Army and had to carry equipment packs through the jungle. When he finally got close to the outskirts of the small town, he laid her down in the woods behind some brush. He didn't want to leave her alone and unconscious, but walking into town with her on his shoulder would arouse too much suspicion.

Once in town, he wandered into the general store. He asked about lodging and found he could rent a cabin on the lake. He booked the most remote one and had a feeling of excitement to be sharing a beautiful scenery with Sam. He then asked to borrow their phone to call for a tow truck.

"Hello, yes. This is Mark Anderson. My wife and I stopped by the side of the road to view some wildlife, and the engine just wouldn't start. It's about five miles out of town."

"Okay, Mark." Rick responded. "How's Sam?"

"It's alright if you can't get to it until tomorrow. The little wife and I are still a bit hung over from the wedding last night and could use a good rest. We've found a quaint little cabin to stay in while the car is getting fixed."

"Sounds good. Keep her out of site. We're getting ready to put the heat on Barker and he might come looking for her."

"I'll call you tomorrow to check on the status of the car. Thanks so much." Mark hung up the phone and smiled at the lady behind the counter. "Thanks for the use of the phone."

"You're on your honeymoon. Congratulations!"

Mark smiled at her knowing that another one of his cons was working like a charm. "We'd like some privacy, if you know what I mean. Can you make sure no one disturbs us?"

"No problem."

Mark then walked around the store and picked up some supplies. He headed over to the cabin to check it out and drop off everything. He pulled back the covers to the bed, closed the curtains, and turned on the lights.

When he made it back to Sam, she was still unconscious. He brushed away the hair that had blown into her face. Mark picked her up into his arms, carried her to the cabin, and placed her onto the bed. Graham had told him to massage her legs every hour for ten minutes to help with circulation. As he massaged her, he looked at her peaceful face. He'd seen many beautiful women over the years, but none compared to Sam. He found himself enjoying massaging her, caressing her legs and feet. When he finished, Mark leaned forward and kissed her on the cheek, remembering the amazing kiss they had shared earlier that day.

He got up, made himself a sandwich, and then went outside to check out the perimeter. The front door of the cabin was facing a lake with a wooden dock. There was also a large window on this side that would allow a spectacular view. The sides had a few smaller windows and the back had none, due to the bathroom being along that wall. The cabin was surrounded by trees and fairly secluded. Mark set up some noise trip lines to alert him to possible visitors. He went back inside and locked the door.

Every hour he massaged Sam and kissed her cheek. The afternoon turned into evening. She was still out. Mark remembered the stories he had heard about her. He remembered the concern Carter, Anthony, and Simon had of that day. It looked like she was going to sleep through it; their concerns were alleviated.

Around eleven pm, Mark climbed into bed next to her and kissed her 'good-night'.

The sun shined brightly into the cabin and woke him up. It was just after six am. He immediately checked on Sam. She was still lying completely still, unconscious. He checked her pulse and forehead; she seemed alright. Mark then started massaging her. When he kissed her, she started to stir. "Sam?"

There was no response.

Another hour passed, Mark took out the supplies to make some breakfast. Sam stirred again. This time, her eyes opened. "Hey, how are you feeling?" He inquired.

"Alright, I think." She smiled at him.

"Are you hungry? I was about to make some eggs."

"Sounds great."

Mark helped her move into a sitting position. He fluffed her pillows and brought her breakfast. "It's not much, but it's editable."

"Thanks. I'm sure it's delicious. I can't even cook."

Mark brought a chair over, so he could eat breakfast with her. He told her what was going on and where they were. "I got you a present. I saw it in the shop yesterday; it make me think of you. It's just a little something, but I hope you like it." He then presented her with a little box.

A smile of delight crossed her face as she looked inside and found a silver butterfly necklace. "It's beautiful. I love it. Thank you."

"Would you like for me to put it on you?"

"Yes, please."

Mark shifted her hair to one side and clasped it. It fell perfectly on her chest.

After Mark redressed her bandages; they spent the remainder of the morning talking. It was amazing how much they had in common. By lunch, Sam was ready to get out of bed. Mark helped her walk over to the table. They spent the afternoon cheating at cards, talking about all sorts of topics, and listening to music on a radio. Mark could tell Sam really liked music. At one point, he asked her if she would like to dance; she wanted to. They danced slowly together, Mark kept her body close to his in case her legs weakened. As they danced, their faces moved closer and closer together. Finally, Mark couldn't resist the temptation any longer. "Would you mind if I kissed you?"

"Please do."

He wasn't sure how long they kissed and danced, but it was magical and he never wanted it to end. Eventually, her legs started giving out, so they sat down again. Mark checked his watch and realized it was getting late; he hadn't touched base with Rick. He gave Sam his gun and headed out to the general store to make the call.

When he returned, Sam was nowhere in sight. Mark became immediately alarmed. Did Barker find her? He rushed over to the bathroom. The door was open; she wasn't inside. He then looked under the bed and checked the closet. She was gone. Mark felt a pain in his heart. He had to find her.

Chapter 10

As he rushed toward the door, he suddenly heard. "Close the door."

Mark recognized the voice and surprisingly looked up. Sam was in the exposed rafters of the vaulted ceiling. "Can you help me down?" She smiled.

She tossed down the gun, and then started climbing toward him. Mark reached up and caught her as she jumped down. He grabbed her in his arms and gave her a deep loving kiss. "You scared me. What took you so long to tell me where you were?"

"You left the door open. I had to make sure you were alone."

Mark had been with many women over the years. He'd lied to them about who he was and what he did. He had to for various reasons. Sam was like no other woman he'd met. He didn't want to pretend to be someone he wasn't. She understood what it was like to be an orphan. She understood what he went through in the war. She understood that every moment was, as she put it, "special and precious", because everything could change in an instant. Sam was the first woman that he'd ever met where he could just be himself. It was refreshing, and the more time he spent with her, the more he craved it. His only concern was that he would fall back into his old habits and lie to her. He couldn't let that happen.

"Sam, I know we've only known each other for just a few days, but I think I'm falling in love with you."

"I don't know what that feels like, but I'm feeling things I've never felt before. It's exhilarating. I like it."

He smiled at her and then leaned in to kiss her again. Sam was right about their situations. Both of them didn't know what tomorrow would bring with him being a criminal of a crime he didn't commit; and her being a soldier fighting a war people thought ended years ago, so they had to make the most of every moment. Tonight, he was going to treasure the time they were allowed to be together. He made them supper and then a fire in the fireplace. He held her, kissed her, and loved her with all his heart.

Sam didn't mind sharing a bed with him. She placed her head on his chest; he wrapped his arms around her and kissed the top of her head. During the night, she started stirring and speaking Vietnamese. Mark woke her up from the nightmare, kissed her gently, and pulled her back into his loving arms. It happened two more times during the night, but Mark didn't mind; it just meant he had more time to cuddle with her.

The following morning, he reluctantly went to call Rick, hoping he would be told they would need another day to take care of Barker, but he wasn't. Rick said they should arrive in time for lunch.

Mark then rented a boat and took Sam out on the

lake. She had been commenting on how pretty it was. He rowed her out to the middle. It was so serene, and she was so beautiful in the sunlight. He kissed her gently, but with a sad heart. Their time together was coming to an end.

Sam must have been feeling the same thing. "I want to invite all of you out to the farm. I'm sure you could use a vacation. You'd still be under my protection and could just relax without worrying about Walters."

Mark gave her a huge smile and kissed her again. "I'd really like that."

"I'm also going to find out what's involved in getting all of you pardoned. I'll do everything I can to clear your names."

Mark was touched beyond belief. "Thank you." He sincerely told her.

Sam smiled her gorgeous smile and leaned in to kiss him again.

They were still in the middle of the lake when the team arrived. Mark rowed them back to shore and helped Sam out of the boat. She rushed over to give Simon a hug.

"Mark, I can see there is something between the two of you. You didn't sleep with her did you?" Rick asked.

"No. We shared the same bed, but we were fully clothed. I wouldn't do that to her. Sam's special."

"Lieutenant, you're not telling me what I think you're telling me?"

"I haven't felt this way about a woman. I really care about Sam. I didn't expect for this to happen, but it has. I don't want to lose her."

Rick gave him a sympathetic smile and a pat on the shoulder.

It was decided that the team would take Sam up on her offer of a vacation. They stopped by Graham's rental car and jumped the battery. After they picked up Graham and Scott at the hotel, they headed for the airport where Max had landed the chopper. Everyone got on Jolly except Rick, who wanted to bring their van, and Scott, who said he'd give the directions during the drive.

They flew to Camp Pendleton where Sam told them to stay aboard while she, Max, and Zach got out. They sat quietly as the blades to the chopper were folded for transport, and it was loaded into the belly of a C-141 Starlifter. Once the cargo door was closed, Graham lead them into another section of the plane set up like a lounge area. Mark sunk down into one of the green sofas.

It dawned on him that this was the plane they flew in on their missions to and from Vietnam. The Beluga was a very comfortable ride. He could hear Billy and Max in the cockpit talking about airplanes. He watched Sam's interactions with her team. The group was very jovial, laid back. It reminded him of how well his team knew each other, like family.

At one point, Zach asked Sam if she was ready for a challenge. Zach was going to play a song she had never heard before and she had to play it perfectly the first time. The bet was doing each other's chores on the farm for a week. Sam was keen. The next thing he knew, "Piano Man" by Billy Joel was playing over the plane's speakers. Sam just smiled. "Is that the best you can come up with? This is going to be like taking candy from a baby." She then pulled out her harmonica and played the bit perfectly. Sam smiled and teased. "Looks like there are no chores for me. Thanks, Zach."

"That's not the part I wanted you to play." Zach gave her a playful look.

Sam laughed. "What part did you expect me to play? That's the only instrument we have with us."

"I suggest you check your cargo more carefully, General." He then walked over to the side of the plane and pulled a tarp. Underneath was a piano.

Sam started laughing. "I don't believe it. Here, move it to the middle of the plane and secure it. I want to play facing everyone." Once that was done, she said, "Play the song again, I wasn't listening to the piano part."

Zach chuckled. "Like hell you weren't. You only get to hear the song once; those are the rules. However, I'll humor you and throw in a second listening."

After he played it the second time, Sam began playing the piano with the song. Mark was amazed that she could catch on so quickly; she had an amazing talent. While playing the instrumental, she suddenly let out a sound of frustration as she missed a note. A smile was on her face as she shook her head and kept playing. At the end, she conceded that Zach had won the competition and asked him to play the song again. This time, she played it perfectly.

The guys started making song requests. Sam played and sang for them. Some of the songs he recognized; others were pieces she had written. Mark was so wrapped up in the beautiful music and her incredible voice that he was surprised when Graham commented to Simon. "It's starting."

"How can you tell?"

"Look at her eyes."

Mark suddenly become more aware of his surroundings. Sam's eyes had a glossed over look. Graham, Simon, and Zach were intensely watching her. Simon moved over to sit next to her on the piano bench. The lyrics of the songs started getting more passionate. Sam was no longer taking requests, but playing whatever she wanted like she was wrapped up in her own world. At one point, she suddenly stopped playing and just stared at the keys.

"Sam, are you going to play another song?" Graham asked her.

"You won't like it." She said looking up at him with a dark, intense look in her eyes.

"Play it anyway." He challenged her.

As Sam started to play, Mark found himself being mentally transported back to Vietnam, back to the war. The song was disturbing, haunting. It brought back memories of things Mark never wanted to remember. It felt like he was back there in the trenches, fighting for his life. People around him being killed, bombs going off.

He didn't know when the song stopped, but

Graham's words brought him back to reality. "I promise I won't stop you, but let me sanitize it first, so you don't get an infection."

Mark looked over at Sam and saw her holding a knife. She had a deep, dark look on her face. She was staring right at Graham who was holding out his hand to take the knife from her. Sam handed him the knife. Graham wiped it down with some disinfectant and handed it back to her. He then asked. "Where are you putting it?"

Sam pointing to the underside of her left arm between her elbow and wrist. Graham wiped down her arm.

Mark was then shocked to see her take the knife and start cutting her arm. He looked around the plane, no one was moving to stop her. Why not? He wanted to help her, but they knew her better than he, so he did nothing. It hurt to watch her carve up her arm. Mark thought she looked like she had gone completely crazy. When Sam was done, the name "Paul" could be seen on her arm. She then wiped the knife off on her pants, turned back to the piano, and started playing again with blood trickling down on the keys and her clothes. No one moved. Everyone was watching.

The next song was beautiful. It was about not crying when someone says good-bye to you. As she got deeper into the song, Mark noticed her breath was starting to strain. She sung a lyric about someone screaming. Tears started pouring down her cheeks. Simon wrapped his arm around her shoulder. She tried to keep singing the song, but was becoming more and more choked up. Simon grabbed her as she completely lost it. He held her tightly. A few minutes passed as she was completely consumed with the outpouring of loss. Tears were welling up in Simon's eyes. Eventually she started to calm down. "It was all my fault." She told Simon.

Simon started to cry and held her tightly. "No, it wasn't. I was there. It was just a horrible accident."

"I set the wire. I killed him."

"No, Sammy. You were protecting him. You were protecting all of us. Charlie was crawling all over the place. The tripwire had to be there, or we could've all been killed. Paul didn't understand. He was lucky. Sam. He had no idea there was a war going on. He was running around, smiling, playing. He died happy."

"I should've been able to save him." She choked out through the tears. "I wasn't fast enough. I knew where the line was. I should have never let him get that far away from me."

"I was not your fault. You were almost killed in the blast. If you had died, we probably wouldn't have made it out of Vietnam alive. The kids definitely wouldn't have. All the POWs you've saved probably wouldn't have made it out either."

"I keep seeing it over and over in my head. I can hear Keyla's screams. I can see his body blown apart. It's my fault. He'd be here today. He could've grown up on the farm. I could've protected him, taken care of him." At that point, she completely lost it again. These cries were even more violent, her entire body was shaking.

Mark felt completely helpless.

A few more minutes passed before she gained a

little bit of control again. She moved away from Simon, got on her knees on the floor, and put her hands behind her head. She was in the position you would put a prisoner in. It reminded Mark of the people they had captured in Nam. Tears were pouring down her cheeks. "Shoot me, Graham! Please!" She started screaming, begging.

Mark was shocked to see Graham take out a gun. He raised it, aimed, and fired. Sam fell silent.

Chapter 11

Simon caught Sam before she hit the floor. Mark's entire body was gripped with sadness. His heart felt broken like she was really gone. Simon carried her over to one of the sofas. Graham rushed over and immediately started attending to her cut arm. Mark also moved over to check on her.

"It worked." Zach commented. "We got her to go over the edge."

"Yeah." Graham sighed.

"You did that to her on purpose?" Mark asked in disbelief feeling very protective of her.

"Yes. She's safe here with us." Zach told him. "Our biggest fear is that she will lose it and be alone. We fear what she might do to herself."

"What did you hit her with?" Mark inquired.

"A tranquilizer dart." Graham quietly answered. "As much as she needs to psychologically release what she keeps bottled up inside, I'm not going to make her suffer. She suffers enough as is."

The next hour was very quiet, a stark contrast to the previous hour. Mark got the impression everyone was lost in their own thoughts. He definitely was. He wanted to see the smiling, beautiful woman he'd spent time with. He wanted to hold her, and love her. All he could do right now was stare at her sleeping face. She looked very peaceful; he was grateful for that.

Sam started to stir. She opened her eyes. "How long was I out?" She asked as she tried to sit up.

Graham helped her. "About an hour."

"How bad was it?"

"Not bad; we've seen worse."

"Thanks, Graham, for everything." She smiled and hugged him.

"Anytime. We're all here for you. We all love you."

The remainder of the flight was light hearted conversation over a poker game. It was like nothing had happened. Sam was smiling and herself again. Mark enjoyed cheating with her.

UTAH

When they landed, Mark found himself on a private landing strip.

"Welcome to UTAH." Sam told them.

Mark gave her a strange look. "I thought you lived in Georgia?"

She smiled. "It's the name of the farm."

"That's a strange name." Billy commented.

"It's so no one can find it." She told him. "Gentlemen, you have over seven hundred acres to relax and be protected. If you leave the farm, your protection ends."

There was a five-foot-ten, white man with black

hair around Mark's age waiting for them with a huge smile on his face. Sam walked over to him with an equally big smile. Their embrace reminded Mark of the heartfelt exchange between Anthony and Sam.

Simon walked over to the man. They shook hands. "Hi Sarge."

"It's good to see you, Simon."

The Sarge then walked over to Graham, Zach, and Max, individually thanking them for bringing Sam home. He then introduced himself to the Mark and Billy. "Hi, I'm Jack Anderson. Welcome to our home."

Mark learned that Max and Zach weren't only best friends, but also roommates. They shared a three-bedroom house that looked tiny compared to the enormous hangar that was its next door neighbor. It seemed that Scott and his family lived on the edge of the property; and Graham had his own house also along the edge, but in the opposite direction. The guys all headed toward their prospective homes, while the Billy and Mark climbed aboard a jeep driven by Jack.

They rode over a hill and saw a two story, yellow farm house that looked like something out of a dream. It had a staircase that lead up to a big wrap around porch. There was a flagpole in front of the house with the American and POW/MIA flags flapping in the wind. Flowers bloomed around the base of the pole.

A young, Vietnamese woman came running down the stairs and straight over to Sam. "Samay," She called out and gave her a huge hug. The two of them spoke a moment in Vietnamese, before Sam introduced her. "This is Keyla, my sister."

"Welcome to our home." She politely greeted

them. “It’s good to see you again, Simon-san.”

“I have been craving your famous Bún riêu.”

She smiled. “Jack told me you were coming. I have some ready for you in the kitchen. Come.”

Simon started to follow her toward the house. “Keyla, you’re the best.”

“Who’s the guy on the porch giving us the death stare?” Billy inquired.

Mark looked at the young, Vietnamese man who was leaning against a column. He had a bandage around his head. The look he was giving them sent a chill up Mark’s spine.

“That’s my brother, Chang.”

“He looks like he’s plotting a way to kill us.” Mark joked.

“I’m sure he’s already come up with half-a-dozen by now.” Sam simply replied. She then turned to Jack. “Where are Won and My?”

“Since you had company coming, they went out on patrol to make sure the perimeter is secure. Shall we show our guests where they are staying?”

They walked around the farm house and discovered a second house not far away. There was a beautiful, big oak tree in the front yard. This house was also two stories, but it was made of red brick with black shutters on the windows and an unusual grey, metallic looking front door. Mark was happy to discover it had four bedrooms and two full bathrooms upstairs. The downstairs was very comfortable looking as well. Mark could tell he was going to enjoy this vacation. The farm seemed very relaxing and quiet.

The front door burst open and a teen-aged,

Vietnamese girl rushed in. She was as beautiful as Keyla and looked a lot like her. “Samay!” She cried as she hurried over to give Sam a kiss on the cheek and a bear hug. “I’m so glad you’re home.”

“It’s good to be home.” Sam sincerely replied. “How was school?”

“I got an A on my math test.” She grinned.

“That’s great, Annie!”

“Yeah, I think all of Max’s tutoring is finally starting to pay off. I’m going to go find him and show him the paper.” With that, she waved ‘good-bye’, told them welcome to the farm, and bolted back out the door.

Sam then turned back to them. “Make yourself at home. The white phone in the kitchen is a direct line to the farm house. Give us a call if you need anything. Supper will be at eighteen-hundred. I suggest you come hungry; Keyla is used to feeding a small army.”

The evening was very jovial. They all sat at a group of picnic tables under the shade of some oak trees. With the exception of Scott, everyone they had met so far was there with the addition of a boy and girl who were in their late teens. They were Vietnamese; the family resemblance between all of them was very strong.

While the dinner was very relaxing, it was also strange. The majority of the conversations were in Vietnamese or a mixture of English and Vietnamese. The meal was also all Vietnamese food. Sam hadn’t been joking about the amount of food her sister prepared; there was plenty. It was as good as Simon had claimed.

Around 8pm, Sam suddenly turned to Graham and said, "I'm ready to go to bed."

Mark could see the exhaustion on her face. He thought back over the day; it had been a long one. She told everyone 'good-night' and gave Jack a hug. The Vietnamese kids all started gathering the dishes. Simon, Max, and Zach helped them.

Billy and Mark were left alone with Jack. "I need to talk to you guys in private. I wasn't expecting Sam to bring back company. That's not to say that you aren't welcome, because you are; but tomorrow something is happening that Sam's not going to be happy about. You don't know our family, don't understand everything that is going on. I am asking you to support my decision and not let Sam convince you otherwise. It is for her protection that I am doing this. I see the way she looks at you Mark, and how you look at her. There is obviously something between the two of you. Please, I'm asking you to first, not to let on that you know anything. If one of the kids finds out, they will go straight to Sam. Second, support my decision."

"What exactly are you asking us to support?" Mark asked.

"I'm clipping her wings. No more missions to Vietnam. No more being a Ghost Soldier. Sam is a daughter to me; I want her to have a normal life. I'm sending the Lihn Ma on a new mission; I want them all to go to college. The Marine Corps will pay for them.

The rest of our unit has been saving up to help pay for Keyla to go too, and Annie once graduates high school."

"We'll back you up." Mark reassured him. "We'll also give you back the ten thousand dollars Sam paid us to help her rescue Simon. Use the money toward their college."

"Thank you."

Simon, Max, and Zach came back out of the house and joined them. "You guys ready for tomorrow?" Jack inquired.

"Yeah, Zach and I are heading out a dawn. We should be back by supper."

"Good." Jack told Max.

"What do you want me to do, Sarge?" Simon asked.

"I'm going to take watch tonight, so I need you up the morning to make sure everything is business as usual."

"You got it."

Graham walked back out of the house. Jack turned to him, "How much did you hit her with?"

"Nothing. She fell asleep while I was changing her bandages. There's a syringe in the top drawer of the dresser. If things get rough, use it. It will knock her out for at least eight hours."

The following day had been wonderful. Sam had taken them horseback riding around the farm. Mark really enjoyed spending time with her. The farm was so peaceful and relaxing. They arrived back at the barn around 5pm and started unsaddling the horses.

"Kelly!" Sam suddenly exclaimed and took off running toward a blonde haired, blue eyed man walking toward them. Next to him was a Hispanic man. They were both around Mark's age and were wearing huge grins.

"Hey, little sister." He greeted her with bear hug.

"Paz." She called to the Hispanic man.

He also gave her a hug. They all exchanged a type of hand jive.

"What are you guys doing here?"

"The Sarge thought it would be nice to have a type of family reunion."

They all walked back to the farmhouse where LT and Carter were waiting with Simon and Jack.

Sam was grinning from ear to ear. Mark could tell she was really happy seeing all of them. She insisted on having a family picture. Billy offered to take it. As Mark watched them, he thought about the picture he'd seen of all of them together in Vietnam. There was no denying the bond that was shared between them.

Their van pulled down the driveway. Rick and Scott had arrived. What perfect timing. Sam then wanted an entire family picture taken on the front steps to the farm house. It included all the guys from her original unit, all the kids, Scott, Graham, Max, and Zach. Billy snapped numerous pictures of them.

That evening felt like a party. Dinner was blessed by Kelly, who had come back from Vietnam and become a minister. After they were all stuffed with

Keyla's amazing cooking, the music began. Sam and Graham pulled out guitars, Won got on some drums, and Zach ran the mixer. They could really jam and played a combination of songs he knew and others he'd never heard before. He wondered how many of the unfamiliar songs were written by Sam. Her family seemed to know the words to most of them. All the songs were upbeat, unlike some of the pieces she played coming back on the plane. Sam was smiling the entire time and seemed to be really enjoying herself. Some of the guys got up and danced with her sisters.

The music started winding down just after ten. At the end of the last piece, Sam turned to them and said. "As much as I love seeing all of you, what's the real reason you're here?"

Chapter 12

"I've called a family meeting." Jack simply told her.

Rick motioned for the team to leave. Mark looked back at Sam wondering how she was going to handle what Jack was getting ready to tell her. He hadn't known Jack for long, but he could tell Jack was one of the most genuine, decent guys he'd ever met. It was obvious how much he cared about Sam; and she cared about him. There was also a form of respect between them.

The following morning, Rick asked, "Hey, guys. Have you noticed the walls and windows to this house?"

"Not really, why?" Mark responded looking up from his newspaper. The Wall Street Journal was his favorite read. Keyla had brought him one with breakfast.

"They are thicker than regular walls. I noticed the farmhouse has normal walls, but this house is different. I find it a bit odd. Also, I drove first on the way here. Scott took over in Colorado Springs. The next thing I knew, I was waking up while we pulled up the drive to the farm. The amount of time that passed makes sense, but I've checked the van's odometer. It's only gone 1,073 miles. There's no way we're in Georgia. Billy, you were in the cockpit. Did you notice anything when you flew here?"

"No, we were above the clouds most of the time. Max had it on autopilot; we were talking and looking at flying magazines. I wasn't really paying attention to the gauges."

"Add that with the fact that all the vehicles have government plates."

"You're not suggesting what I think you're suggesting. Are you?" Mark asked starting to get an uneasy feeling.

Rick told them. "Guys, do you realize that we don't actually know where we are. I'm getting the feeling we're on a top secret military base. We could be in big trouble."

"Sam is protecting us. Everything she's done has been to help us. Why would she turn us in now?"

"Mark, you're smitten with her. You aren't thinking clearly. I'm just saying that until we are 100% certain she is on our side; we need to be cautious."

After Mark finished reading his paper, Rick walked with him over to the main house. Rick wanted to take a closer look around. Mark wanted to see Sam.

Zach and Max were sitting on the front porch polishing several pairs of shoes, laughing at the scene in the front yard. Mark and Rick joined them to watch. "What's going on?" Rick inquired while looking at Sam, Chang, Won, and My who were lined up next to each other. Scott was barking orders. After each command, he and Graham would walk up to the kids and make the necessary adjustments.

Zach jovially replied, "The kids have never worn their uniforms. Scott's teaching them the proper protocols of how to salute and stand."

Rick leaned back in one of the rockers. "This ought to be entertaining."

They had been watching for about ten minutes when suddenly Zach and Max were on their feet and standing at attention. "General Wentworth, Sir."

"As you were, Captains." A gray haired, white man responded. Mark had been so wrapped up in watching Sam, he hadn't noticed when the man joined them on the porch. "After this is over, I want the two of you to take a walk with me."

"Yes, Sir." They responded in unison.

The General then turned to Rick. "Major Peters, I hope you and your men are enjoying your vacation."

"We are, thank you."

"Glad to hear it." He replied before walking down the front steps and over to the group practicing. They all saluted him. Mark couldn't make out what he was saying as he shook each of their hands, but he couldn't miss the hug he gave Sam.

At eleven hundred hours, the ceremony began. Mark and his friends sat in the audience with the families. Jack, Lt. Anthony, and the remainder of the men from Sam's original unit in Vietnam were all dressed in their military uniforms. There were numerous awards given to Sam's team.

Sam was the last one honored. It was a strange contrast. Mark was twenty-two when the Army sent him off to fight in Vietnam. Here was Sam, the same age, being awarded the Medal of Honor, the Vietnam Service Medal, the Purple Heart, and the Prisoner of War Medal. Everyone stood and saluted her. Mark smiled as he looked at a true American hero.

That day, General Sam Anderson, Lt.Col. Scott Russell, Major Graham Martin, Captain Chang Quach, 1st Lt. Won Quach, and 2nd Lt. My Quach retired.

Just after lunch the following day, Max walked into the farmhouse wearing a flight suit. Sam looked up from the poker game they were playing. "Where are you going?"

"General Wentworth wants Baby taken to Dobbins. I thought you might like to go with me on one last flight. I spoke to Scott; he said he'd fly your Barron there to bring us back. I have a full tank of gas, so we don't have to go straight there." He smiled. "Go put your flight suit on and come with me."

"Okay," She told him putting down her cards. A few minutes later, she was back downstairs wearing the green jumpsuit.

Mark rode with them over to the hanger. Out on the tarmac was a shiny, black fighter jet. Mark had never seen anything like it. Sam was walking around the plane, running her hands down the wings and body. At one point, she stopped and it looked like she was hugging it. Mark realized she loved the plane and was saying 'goodbye' to it.

"Hey, Sam." Max called to her as he walked out of the hanger with two helmets. As she looked over to him; he tossed her the keys. "You fly her, one last time."

Sam gave him a sad smile. "Thanks, Max."

They put their helmets on, climbed aboard, and Sam fired up the jets. Shortly after takeoff, she rolled the plane. A few minutes later, she flew over the runway upside down. Mark stood and watched the aerobatic show she put on. He smiled as he learned something new about her; she obviously loved to fly.

While she was away, he asked Simon about Sam and her siblings. Simon said, "The kids are very close. There is no selfishness among them, always giving to help each other. They never fight, partially due to the unspoken hierarchy between them. Despite this hierarchy, they treat each other with respect. Everyone knows their place; everyone does their part. Sammy is closest to Chang; he's second in command. Chang is incredibly protective of her. She knows she can count on him, no matter what."

Mark thought about his comment and it explained some of the things he had seen.

A couple of days passed. Sam's extended family had left back to their homes. Mark really enjoyed the laid back lifestyle; and the hospitality of Sam's family was starting to make the farm feel like home. He and Billy strolled up the front steps and into the house.

"Keyla, where are they?" Mark could hear the panic in Jack's voice. "Where are my kids? Please tell me they didn't go back to Vietnam? I know they went back that week they just disappeared. It's more than a coincidence that it happened only days after Lt. Mags got out of prison for serving only three years for massacring your entire family. I'm sure Max and Zach helped without knowing what was going on. Sam's too smart for that. I don't believe Sam killed Mags, but I can imagine in my most horrific nightmares what Chang did to that man. I know they will never tell what happened, and I'm positive the body will never be found. What I do know is that Chang came back a less angry kid. I stopped worrying he was going to suddenly kill every American he could. Keyla, please, I don't want them going back. They've sacrificed enough. It's time they were allowed to live normal lives."

"Normal? What kind of life do you think they'll be able to live? You're asking them to stop doing what they've been doing their entire lives. Jack, you can take them out of Vietnam, but you can't take Vietnam out of them. It's who they are."

"Sam's barely spoken to me. Please Keyla..." He pleaded with her.

"What do you expect? You did to her what her real dad used to do to her all the time."

"What?!"

"You forced her to do something she didn't want to do. What's even worse, is that you got the entire unit to stand behind you. Sam trusted you. She trusted all of you. You were her family."

"We are her family. We're protecting her. It's no different from how she protects you. Keyla, please..."

"You should've talked to her instead of going

behind her back." She paused and then quietly said. "It's Tuesday. They're at the combat zone doing what they do every Tuesday."

Jack looked relieved. "I just have this horrible feeling that I'm going to turn around, and they'll be gone. Sam's been too quiet about all of this; too accepting. I know the transition will be difficult for them, and it's going to take time. I just can't shake this feeling that they are going to sneak off to Vietnam, and I'm going to lose them for good."

Keyla gave him a sympathetic hug. She then turned to Mark and said, "Hello, how are you?"

"I'm good, thanks." Mark told her.

Billy added, "We couldn't help but overhear, what's the combat zone?"

She smiled. "I'll take you."

They rode in the jeep to a part of the farm they hadn't seen. When they came around the bend, Mark saw a beautiful lake. The sun was glistening off the water. There was a splash and then laughter. Mark looked around, but only saw Won in the water. He then looked way up into the trees and saw the other three. They were standing on two-by-four boards that connected the trees together. Sam was wearing a tank top and shorts which showed off her perfectly toned body. In her hands was a Jahng Bong. Chang and My also held Jahng Bongs as they moved in to confront her. Sam quickly moved her bare feet across the board in an aggressive maneuver. Mark watched as the staffs struck each other in combat. The kids were good, really good. He was very impressed with how well they balanced and did acrobatics while fighting.

The battle waged on for about ten minutes when Sam suddenly did a backflip. Her feet landed slightly crooked; Mark could tell she was off balance. Two more back flips followed as she jumped off the board and dove into the water. When she came up, she was laughing and calling back up to them in Vietnamese.

Sam climbed out of the lake and walked straight toward Mark. Her clothes clung tightly to her perfect body. "Hi, having fun watching?"

"I sure am." He pulled her into his arms and gave her a long, deep kiss.

When they finally broke from the embrace, Mark thought he saw her blush. He looked around and discovered Chang and My had jumped down and were sitting on the shore with Won, Keyla, and Billy, talking in Vietnamese. He was starting to get used to the fact that there was a lot of Vietnamese spoken there. Some of the words he had learned had even started coming back to him. He also noticed the Lihn Ma all wore the same tattoo on their left shoulders with a slight variation to it.

An alarm rang through the air. The Ghosts took off running.

Chapter 13

"Come with me." Keyla told him and Billy.

"What is that?" Billy asked.

"The fire alarm."

"Why are they running?" Mark asked puzzled. "Wouldn't it be faster to ride back with us?"

"It is quicker to cut across the fields. They will scale and jump the fence. We will have to drive around."

Keyla was right. By the time they arrived at the farm house, Sam's group had already left for the fire at a neighboring farm. As she drove, Keyla explained that they were part of the volunteer fire department.

Mark couldn't help but noticed the massive iron gate they passed through as they left the farm for the first time. The land didn't look much different from Sam's place, but he definitely noticed Georgia plates on the cars.

When they arrived, he heard Max yelling. "Sam, get out of there! We've gotten all the people out. The place is going to go."

Mark ran over to Zach. "What can I do to help?"

"Watch the kids. They'll know what Sam's doing; they think as one. Go help them."

Chang and Won were climbing a tree. Mark and

Billy hurried over to My who was standing underneath one of the tree's branches. "What can we do?" Billy asked.

"I need for you to crisscross your arms, like this." They copied her.

"What's happening?" Mark inquired, worried about Sam.

"We expect her to jump off the roof. She had to go upstairs."

Sure enough, things started being thrown out of an upstairs window: a fire jacket, an oxygen mask, shoes. Sam then climbed out of the window and headed toward the roof. Max, Zach, and Graham joined them in crossing their arms. Chang was now hanging upside down in the tree with Won laying across his legs.

Sam took off running across the ridge of the roof. She jumped off doing a front flip. Chang yelled something in Vietnamese causing Sam to reach for him. He caught her wrists, but one slipped loose as the tree branch dipped down from the sudden weight, and Sam swung forward. They both reached again. This time he grabbed her successfully. It was like something out of an acrobatics show. Mark watched as Sam's swinging slowed down. The kids then did a countdown and Sam did a backflip, landing into the human net made by their crossed arms.

"Thanks." She told them and then turned to Graham adding. "I'll be right back."

The sound of the cracking and collapsing of the entire house didn't seem to faze Sam as she took off across the front yard. Mark, Max, and Zach followed her, curious as to what she was doing.

There was a little girl around the age of six standing with her parents, crying. Sam walked up to her and dropped to her knees to become more eye level with her. She started unbuttoning her shirt. Mark hadn't even noticed she'd changed into the shirt with jeans. Once the top was open, she untied some cloth that was tied around her waist. Sam unrolled it revealing five tiny puppies. The little girl smiled and threw her arms around Sam.

"That's why she's the best at search and rescue." Mark heard Zach comment to Max.

"Yep. She could find a needle in a haystack."

Sam then turned toward them. "Are you alright?" Mark asked.

"Yeah. I need to see Graham. Come on."

Mark followed her over to an ambulance where Graham was waiting with bags of ice for her feet. Graham then started giving her a through exam. "Chang's death grip broke your watch. You're going to have a massive bruise under it." He made her take off her shirt and checked every suture on her back. She was going to be fine. Graham joked, "I'm convinced you can't feel half the nerves on your body anymore."

That evening, the guys were watching TV in the guest house when metal shades suddenly covered the windows and they heard locks locking. Rick was immediately on his feet and at the front door. "We're locked in. I don't like this, at all."

They checked all the windows and both doors. Being trapped in the house was very unsettling. “I told you there was something strange about this place. We’re trapped and could easily be arrested.”

“Rick, do you really think Sam would have us arrested now? She’s had plenty of opportunities including when we were trapped by Walters. Why would she do it now?”

“I don’t know, but it really bothers me that we don’t actually know where we are.”

Mark shot Billy a look. They did know where they were and hadn’t told Rick.

Tension was rising as the guys tried everything they could think of to get out of the house. About ten minutes passed with no luck. Mark couldn’t believe Sam would double cross them, but Rick had made a valid point.

They heard a sound coming from the closet. Mark cautiously opened the door. To their surprise, the carpet started moving and lifted completely up. Annie’s head appeared as she started climbing out of the hole in the floor. “We’re under lockdown. Samay sent me to get you out of here.”

“What caused the lockdown?”

“I don’t know, but we must hurry. I have weapons for you. Come on.”

They climbed down the ladder into an underground tunnel. Mark watched as Annie closed the hole she had made in the floor. The tunnel was lit with regular lights and some strange red lights. Annie handed each of them a machine gun.

“Where’s yours?” Billy asked.

"I don't know how to use one. Samay didn't want me to be a soldier."

Billy took the point with Annie giving directions where to turn. The tunnel system was a massive maze with no directional signs. Mark figured you could easily get lost for days if you didn't know where you were going.

A loud explosion was heard from above. Annie screamed and dropped to her knees with her hands covering her head. She was trembling in fear.

"Don't worry." Mark told her. "I'm not going to let anyone hurt you. You just stay right next to me."

They continued their evacuation turning this way and that. Mark wondered how far they had actually walked. All of a sudden, Annie stopped. "It's over."

"How can you tell?" Mark asked.

"The lights aren't red anymore."

Looking at the walls, Mark noticed all the lights were the same yellow color. Annie turned down another tunnel and then took them up a ladder. He was surprised to discover they were in the hangar. Sam was waiting for them, smiling. "Everyone alright?" Annie ran to her sister. Sam grabbed her tightly in her arms and kissed her cheek. "I told you to trust them to protect you. You're okay." She softly told her sister.

"What caused the lockdown?" Rick inquired.

"I owe you all an apology. It was a drill that only I knew about. You see, we can't actually practice with the real people we're protecting, because then they will know we have the tunnels running throughout the farm. You provided the perfect opportunity to run a house rescue drill and a night defensive. I would appreciate it if you would understand that we can't tell you where you actually are. It's a matter of national security as well as keeping my family safe."

"Your secret is safe with us." Rick told her.

Once they were back in the guest house, alone, Rick commented, "Guys, I get the feeling there was more than one test happening tonight. Did you see the way Sam was holding her sister? It was a protective stance purposefully keeping Annie's back to us."

"Rick," Mark commented. "Stop being paranoid. You're starting to act crazy like Billy."

"I'm just saying, I think we were tested. I also think we passed the test."

The following day, Mark couldn't help but notice The Ghosts were friendlier towards them. Even Chang had stopped giving them his death stares. Mark had to admit that Rick's hunch may have been right.

Mark woke up to another beautiful, sunny day. It had been a couple of days since the lockdown. The farm was so peaceful, so quiet. He could definitely get used to this. After he got dressed, he wandered over to the main house to have breakfast and see Sam. Keyla told him that she wasn't home, so he grabbed the newspaper and some coffee, and headed out to sit on the front porch.

About an hour passed when Scott's car pulled up

in front of the house. He was still on his crutches, so it took him a few minutes to get up the steps. He came over to sit and chat with Mark. Shortly after that, Simon came outside. "Have either of you seen Sammy? Jack hasn't seen her or any of The Ghosts all morning."

Neither one of them had, but Scott told him. "Sam told me to be here for an important meeting. Tell Jack to wait here, he'll see her soon."

They went back to talking. A short while later, Zach arrived with his military boxes hanging over his shoulders. It reminded Mark of that first morning he met him. Zach rushed up the stairs and into the house. Scott followed. Mark thought this seemed very curious, so he decided to check it out.

He suddenly heard arguing. He rushed inside and discovered Jack had Zach pushed up against the wall. "Where are my kids, Zach?"

Zach winced. Mark remembered he was wounded, somewhere on his torso. "You know I can't tell you that. It's classified."

"They are retired. Please tell me they didn't go back to Vietnam."

"I don't like this any more than you do. But I'm under orders from Washington. Now, let me go, so I can do my job."

With that, Jack released him. The look on his face told Mark something was terribly wrong.

Mark sat on the sofa wondering where Sam was and what she was doing that was so dangerous. He watched Zach and Scott set up the equipment. Jack had also sat down. They watched and waited.

Zach turned on the mobile command station. It was the most amazing combination of military equipment Mark had ever seen. He wondered what all it could do.

"We're connected to the satellite." Zach announced. "Max, can you hear me?"

"Loud and clear."

"I'm going to run the precheck diagnostics. Stand by."

Another few minutes passed. The sound of Zach flipping switches on the console was the only sound in the room.

"You're clear."

"Roger that. I'm filing my flight path. We have six souls on board."

"Zach, is she coming home?" Jack asked.

Zach turned and gave him a sympathetic look. "I don't know."

"Sam stopped her retirement paperwork." Scott told him. "She asked Max to get her as far as the South China Sea. The rest of the way, she was going alone. We wouldn't let her. It was agreed they could go as long as they understood everything was on a 'need to know' basis. Only the kids know what's really going on."

"And they'll never tell us." Jack commented.

The creaking of the screen on the back door was heard. Keyla and Annie entered the room and quietly sat on the sofa with Jack. Simon also joined the group. The mood was ominous.

Zach was intensely studying the console. A few more minutes passed. Mark could hear the ticking of the old clock hanging on the wall. Each tick seemed to make Jack tense a bit more.

"On my mark." Zach said. "5...4...3...2...1. Welcome to Vietnam. The skies are clear of Charlie. You should have a smooth ride."

Now Mark was intensely listening to the radio. Why was Sam in Vietnam? He was starting to feel worried.

Chapter 14

It felt like an eternity before Max came back on the radio. "I have a visual on our target. How's the ground?"

"I'm not detecting any movement. You're clear to set her down."

UTAH - (Vietnam via visual and audio feed.)

A visual came on one of Zach's screens. Mark could see a village that still looked war torn and deserted. He then saw Sam. It was shocking at first. She was wearing an NVA uniform. He then realized, they all were. He smiled at her black hair, remembering the first time he saw her through the binoculars.

"Graham, is it working?"

"The camera is rolling."

"Stay right with me." Sam turned and spoke directly into the camera. "Jack, you have always been there for me. I've been very fortunate to have you as my dad these past ten years. Thank you, for everything you have done for me and the kids. We are very grateful.... I know you're upset with me right now.

I never wanted to hurt you. I need for you to understand; this is something I have to do."

"Come home, Sam." He gently told her.

"I am home. Zach, start recording."

"Recording started."

"This is General Sam Anderson of the U.S. Marines, Special Forces. I am in the village of Son Tay, in the Quang Ngai Province, South Vietnam." She gave the date and time, and then proceeded to walk into the village. Annie and Keyla moved closer to the screen. Keyla sat behind Annie, looking over her shoulder and wrapping her arms around her. "Annie, this is where we were all born. This is our home."

Chang was moving ahead of her, moving things out of the way. Sam walked into a hut and down into a tunnel. Mark remembered sometimes having to go down into the VC tunnels. It always made him feel very uncomfortable. Watching live footage of her crawling through one was disturbing. However, he was impressed with the lighting system they had.

Sam kept narrating; explaining the function of each room. She was smiling and telling stories. It reminded Mark of a family reunion. He got the impression she was really happy. Jack and Simon were reacting, making comments about their memories of being there. Annie was asking questions. She too seemed very happy.

Sam entered another room, a larger one. "Wait." Annie suddenly said, smiling. "I remember this room."

Sam smiled. "This is where you spent most of your time in hiding."

Simon commented. "I remember this room too. This is where I wore out the knees to my pants giving Paul and you piggyback rides."

The tour continued with Sam interacting with them. Every once in a while, Mark could see My or Won doing something in the background, but he couldn't make out what it was. Eventually, the tour made its way to the surface again. Sam squinted her eyes as she entered the sunlight.

The jovial mood between them, then got somber. Mark noticed tears were streaming down Keyla's cheeks. He wasn't sure when they had started. Chang handed Sam a bouquet of flowers. She walked over to the other side of the village and into a hut. Chang, Won, and My entered as well. The flowers were placed down on the ground. Sam knelt to her knees. "Yea, though I walk through the valley of the shadow of death, I will fear no evil; for thou art with me." Sam then leaned down and kissed the ground.

"That's where her mom died." Keyla told Annie. "Chang buried her, gave her a proper Christian burial. Samay's mom was the nicest person you'd ever meet. We all loved being around her. She was a beautiful person. You're named after her."

"Is that why Samay didn't want me to be a soldier?" Annie inquired.

"Samay saved you. There was no need for you to be a soldier. The others had no choice.

"Chang took her father; we don't know what he did with the body. He only told us that he left it for the maggots to eat. Our mother was furious with him, told him that he was a disgrace to the family. You see,

Samay's father was our mom's older brother. Our mother chose not to believe the truth about him. However, when Chang told our father what had happened, he told Chang not to worry about it.

"Chang had been hiding on the edge of the village. He saw Samay kill her father and take off running. He ran after her. He caught up with her in the jungle. She told him about her mother, the promise that was made, and asked him to bury her. She also asked him to take care of Paul. Chang gave her his word. Samay gave Chang her gun and promised to return. Chang helped her clear the brush off the plane and push it out onto the field."

Mark watched Sam get up off her knees. Sam and the kids crossed the village to the edge of the jungle. Chang handed her another bouquet of flowers.

Sam, Chang, Won, and My all knelt to their knees. Sam spread the flowers around the inside of the circle they formed. They joined hands, and along with Keyla, Annie, and Jack, all recited something in Vietnamese. Mark got the impression is was some sort of prayer. They sat in silence. Eventually, Sam kissed the ground.

As the four of them stood up, they embraced in a group hug. It was a touching moment, a private one. They then slowly starting walking back through the village. Keyla was in full, silent waterworks. Tears had also started running down Annie's cheeks.

The room was completely silent. Jack's tense look was exponential from before; Simon also looked worried, scared. What did they know that he didn't?

Sam finished her walk where she had first come onto the screen. "Keyla, it's time."

"We love you, Samay." Annie told her. "Thank you."

"I love you too." She replied with a sad smile. "Take care of each other."

"Come on." Keyla told Annie, before becoming completely choked up. The two sisters quickly left the room. Mark heard the sound of the screen door closing behind them.

Sam gave My a huge bear hug. They shared the tight embrace for a few moments. There was no doubt how close she was to her siblings. When they released the hug, Sam kissed her on the cheek. My somberly walked past the camera and out of sight.

The close moment was repeated individually with Won and Chang. Chang stayed a few extra moments, as they both turned to look at the village. He handed her something; and she pulled off her dog tags and put them around his neck. Chang then turned and walked away.

Tears were now pouring down Jack and Simon's cheeks. It was like they were watching a movie with a sad ending. The main difference, it was their true story about someone they loved. Mark suddenly felt something wet hit his hands. He hadn't realized that he had started crying too. He didn't know her like they did, but he loved her. He didn't want to lose her; he hadn't had enough time with her and now he would never get the chance.

Sam's clothes started flapping in the wind. Mark realized she had signaled Max to start the chopper. He watched as she motioned for him to take it up. The camera footage jolted as the chopper left the ground. However, it seemed to be hovering.

Tears were now pouring down Sam's cheeks. She looked directly into the camera. "On behalf of The U.S. Government and The President of the United States, I hereby officially close the last remaining U.S. base in South Vietnam." With that, she activated the device Chang had handed her.

What followed was a series of explosions that came from the tunnels. Mark watched as her facial expression revealed the pain Sam was feeling as her entire village was blown up and destroyed. She fell to her knees in agony.

"Don't turn around, Sam!" Jack shouted.

Sam motioned for the camera to be turned off.

"Max!" Zach sounded alarmed. "You need to get out of there. You've woken the neighbors. I'm detecting ground and air movement heading your way."

"Roger that. Did you get the feed?"

"I have a copy to send to Washington. General Wentworth has been watching the live feed as well. Now, get out of there!"

"Is Sam on the chopper?" Jack's words jolted Mark. The color had completely drained from his face.

Mark hadn't once thought of that being an option. He then realized the stress and worry Jack had for Sam. With Charlie quickly approaching, what would she do? Was she allowing herself to be killed? Was she choosing to die where her mother and brother died?

Zach didn't answer Jack. He was busy flipping switches on the control panels and monitoring enemy movement. Mark could see a lot of red dots moving toward their location.

"She just opened a hornet's nest." Scott commented. "Zach, what can I do?"

"Watch this screen. Let me know if it gets close to the red. Max, Charlie is approaching at a rapid rate. You may have MiGs. They will be on top of you at any moment."

"Everyone put on your five-point harnesses and hang on." Mark heard Max tell them.

Mark glanced over at Jack, who looked like he was saying a little prayer. No one had answered the question. Was Sam aboard the chopper or still on the ground getting ready to face the troops, alone?

"I have a visual. They are Soviet MiG-21s. We're in trouble." Max told them.

One helicopter versus two MiGs. There were no odds for success; the chopper would lose. "Fly casually, Max." Sam's voice came over the radio. Mark saw Jack sigh with relief, but they were far from safe.

"Zach, clear the line. I'm switching to an NVA channel."

"Sam, your codes are over ten years old."

"They're still codes. We have to try something."

"The line is clear."

Mark heard her speaking Vietnamese over the radio. He also heard someone respond.

"Zach, we're off the channel."

"The MiGs are moving away."

There was silent anticipation. Mark could hear the ticking of the clock as they waited to see what would happen.

"Guys, the MiGs are turning back around." Zach solemnly said.

"What's the status of our weapons?" Sam inquired.

"They're locked and loaded."

"Good. Keep them hidden and stand by."

"Sam, what's the plan?"

"You know the rules. We don't exist. We can't fire upon them unless they fire at us first. We can't cause an international incident."

"One shot and you'll be blown out of the sky."

"Then I suggest you and Max quickly come up with a plan to prevent that from happening."

"How are the turbos looking?" Max asked.

"They're good at the moment. Scott is watching the gauge. You thinking about making a run for it."

"Yeah. What do you think about launching a decoy and immediately going into Omega Theta?"

"We'll have to time it just right. Be ready on my mark."

Zach was intensely watching the monitors. The dead silence was almost more than Mark could bare.

"They have missile lock on you." Zach told them.

"They've just launched. It's headed straight for us." Max replied.

"Hold it. Hold it. Now, Max!" Zach's hand started moving rapidly over the console. There was a loud explosion heard over the radio followed by a second fainter one.

"Great shot, Zach! One MiG down."

"That was the easy part." Zach replied.

Mark was intensely watching the console trying to figure out exactly what was going on. Dials were spinning and moving in an erratic behavior. Zach and Scott seemed to understand what was happening. Mark wished Billy was there to tell him. He thought about how Billy would fly when they were being pursued or shot at. He imagined the helicopter rapidly switching directions and altitude in an attempt to shake off the pursuing fighter jet. Billy would fly down low, hugging the ground. Mark wondered if that was what Max was doing.

"The weapon's array just went out." Zach told them.

"Charlie must have hit it. We're under heavy fire."

"The air speed is borderline in the red." Scott suddenly said.

"You're in too steep of a dive! Pull up!" Zach yelled.

"Not yet. I almost have him right where I want him." Max replied.

"I'm getting warning lights. It's too much stress on Jolly."

"I see the lights." Mark could hear the intensity in Max's voice. "I'm going to pull up...now."

"You're pulling up too steep. You're going to pull Jolly apart."

"I'm trying to get that MiG to crash. Darn, he pulled up just in time."

"Max! Are you spinning?" Zach alarmingly asked.

"Yes."

"You're rapidly losing altitude. 10,000... 9,000... 8,000... 7,000..."

Mark noticed numerous lights flashing on the control panel. This was it. They were spinning out of control with a MiG trying to blow them out of the sky. If the MiG didn't get them, the ground would.

"6,000... 5,000... 4,000... 3,000... 2,000... Max!"

Mark braced himself for the inevitable. Sam was going to die. He silently said. "I love you, Sam."

Chapter 15

The explosion ripped him to his core. Mark buried his face into his hands and began to weep uncontrollably. He couldn't remember the last time he had cried like this. She was gone. His heart physically ached with the pain. Life just wasn't fair. First he came back from war a criminal for following orders. Then, he finally meets the woman of his dreams and she ironically gets killed in Vietnam. He longed to hold her and kiss her one more time. He would do anything to be given that opportunity.

"Zach?" Scott asked.

"Yeah, I see it." He replied.

Mark looked up to see a baffled look on Zach's face.

"Max?"

"Yeah."

"You guys alright?"

"Um...some of us are a little green, but yeah."

"What just happened?" Zach asked.

"Sam did it." Max sounded out of breath. "She ordered the tail spin to knock Charlie off guard. While we were spinning, she climbed down to the rockets. On her mark, we stopped spinning and she manually launched and hit the MiG."

"How did she not fall off?"

"Sam and Chang strapped their parachutes together. Chang's death grip held them both on...Can you tell me which way is home? We've had enough fun for one day."

"Gladly, just do me one favor. The next time you two decide to spin Jolly on purpose, let me know. We thought you were goners."

"Roger that. Sorry man."

UTAH

The following afternoon, Mark watched The Beluga land. As soon as he saw Sam, he ran over to her and kissed her like he'd never kissed a woman before. She tasted so good. "I love you." He told her while he held her tight in his arms. He never wanted to let her go. But he did, so Jack could hug her too. Jack was weeping as he hugged her for a very long time.

Two days later, Mark chased after her when she walked out of the farm house.

"Is it your turn to babysit me?" Sam angrily asked him.

"I was just hoping to spend some time together, just the two of us."

She stopped walking and turned to him. "I'm sorry, Mark. I didn't mean to snap." Her tone was much calmer. "Jack's overprotectiveness is not necessary. I'm not going back to Vietnam. There's nothing to go back to now. My home is gone." She turned away, so he couldn't see her face, but he could tell by the tone in her voice that she was hurting. "Look, spending time with me is not a good idea. I'm not a good person. I kill people. I caused the death of my entire village. I knew the NVA were coming. I didn't warn them; I didn't try to save them. I just ran and left them to die. I can still hear their screams. I've tried to pray like my mom taught me, but I can't ask for forgiveness, because I don't deserve it." She sat down and buried her head into her hands.

Mark sat down next to her. "Yes, you kill people, but only because you have no other choice. You're not a killer. In war, terrible things happen, and you find yourself in situations where you do things that you would never choose to do. I've killed people too. I didn't want to, but I had too. I'm good at using a gun and I still use one, but I don't want to kill anyone. I think you are the same way. You were just a kid when your village was attacked. You couldn't have taken them on by yourself, but your escape allowed you to save many American lives, including mine.

"You have a good heart, Sam Anderson. I wish you could see yourself the way everyone else can see you."

They sat in silence for a long time.

Eventually she said. "I really hurt Jack."

"You scared him; he loves you very much."

"I love him, too. Jack's a great dad. He never liked the arrangement I made with Wentworth."

"How did you meet General Wentworth? You two seem like an unlikely pair."

Sam smiled. "Jack and LT had been trying to get me papers to come to the U.S. It was very difficult since I had no birth certificate and only a video to prove who I was. The time came for Jack, Carter, and Simon to rotate out. Jack immediately reupped for a fourth tour, saying he wasn't going to leave me behind. He thought of me as his daughter. Simon decided to stay and help Jack, and reupped for his second tour. Carter was asked to take the tape and find my grandfather. Maybe he could do something from the U.S. side to get me out.

"A couple of months passed without much word from Carter. It was time for LT, Kelly, and Paz to rotate out. They were all that was left of the original group who knew the truth about me. LT stayed saying Jack was going to need a commanding officer to help him keep me a secret. Paz and Kelly went home.

"One day, a helicopter landed on base and a Marine Corp. general got out. Some of the new guys snickered that he had gotten lost since we were on an Army base. The general asked to speak to me in private. He handed me a birth certificate, U.S. passport, and a letter from my grandfather.

"My grandfather didn't know my mom was in Vietnam or anything about me. They had had a falling out. He was excited to meet me. Carter had found him, here." Sam raised her hands into the air. "This is his farm.

"My grandfather was a retired Colonel. He'd served with General Wentworth in World War Two and Korea; they were close friends. When my grandfather saw the video my mom had made, he picked up the phone and called Wentworth. Carter says Wentworth was here by the next day.

"Wentworth told me to grab my things; I was going back to the U.S. with him. I told him about Jack, Simon, LT, and the kids. I told him I wasn't leaving them behind, so I proposed leading rescue missions to save the POWs. I knew Chang, Won, My, and I could get onto the NVA bases. I had given them the same tattoo Ho Chi Minh had given me; I had just adjusted their ranks on the tattoo. As far as Charlie was concerned, we were NVA, part of the children's army.

"Wentworth said we'd work it out. The following day, Jack, LT, and Simon received orders that they were going home. We boarded the chopper together and flew to Son Tay to pick up the kids.

"We were in a plane over the Pacific when Wentworth was notified that my grandparents had been killed in a car crash. He then decided to change some of the official paperwork. You see, my grandfather's first name was Sam. So, Wentworth changed my grandfather's status to active duty and promoted him to general. I operate as him and report only to General Wentworth.

"After landing at Camp Pendleton, we stayed for a couple of months sorting out details and picking men to join my newly created unit. However, tension was high on the base. It wasn't exactly ideal having five Vietnamese children there. You remember what it was like when you first came back. People hated the soldiers, called them baby killers; and the soldiers hated the Vietnamese.

"So, we moved here. It gave us plenty of space to have a base as well as allow us to be away from the public. Jack adopted all of us. He put up with so much crap that first year. People hated us. It definitely wasn't what I was expecting having listened to stories from the guys about what their home was like.

"Jack was told we had to go to school, so he enrolled us. It didn't go well. Chang was in a fight within the first five minutes. I, of course, came to his aid. Chang hated being here. He hated Americans for killing his family; the other kids kept their emotions more under control. After the third fight in one week, Chang and I were expelled. We used to walk the others to school to protect them. People were mean and cruel to them, and I wasn't going to put up with it. They didn't deserve it; they'd done nothing wrong. Jack and Simon also got into arguments and fights protecting them. The barn was burned down. I think the only reason they didn't burn the house was out of respect for my grandfather.

"Jack finally said we weren't allowed to leave the farm without him or Simon with us. Chang wasn't allowed to leave at all. Then, one day, everyone started getting sick. The flu was going around. We ran out of food. Jack had taught me how to drive, so I took Chang, Won, and My into town to buy soup and crackers for the family.

"I was the only one who could control Chang. I had told him we weren't getting into any fights. We had made it through the grocery with just a few stares and name calling. Chang was under control. We started heading back to the farm when I saw a fire in the hotel.

There were four children in a fifth floor window. They were trapped; the ladders weren't long enough to reach them. Time was of the essence; the Ghost Soldiers sprang into action.

"We climbed to the roof of the building next door and jumped across. We climbed down to the window and put the children on our backs. After saving the children, we headed back to our Jeep to discover all the tires had been slashed and the food was thrown all over the ground. Chang asked why I had brought them to this horrible country. He and Won picked up all the food. My had twisted her ankle during the rescue, so I put her on my back, and we started walking the fifteen miles back to the farm.

"We were a couple of klicks out of town when a truck pulled up and stopped. We all went on alert to defend ourselves. The guy suddenly said "I mean you no harm" in Vietnamese. He sat down on the ground and told me that I looked like my mother. They had been steady sweethearts until she decided to become a missionary. He had been back from Nam a couple of months and while he was really angry to find 'gooks' in his hometown and he hated us; he had seen our rescue and realized he'd been wrong. We were told that we had made a friend that day, and if he could accept us, the town could too, in time.

"We were asked to join the Volunteer Fire Department. I accepted. We rode in the back of his truck to the farm. Later that afternoon, the Jeep showed up with four new tires. It took a long road to get to where we are now. Jack stuck with us through all of it. I would never intentionally hurt him."

"I can't believe after all these years, you are still rescuing POWs."

"There were numerous missions at first; we rescued you on our third. After President Nixon negotiated the release of hundreds of prisoners, we thought our job would be over. However, when I reconciled the list of prisoners rescued with the national POW/MIA list; we were still missing a few people. I had already planted numerous listening devices all of the country. We continued to monitor the chatter and found more missing men to rescue. At the same time, I didn't want my unit to be dissolved, because it would be harder to sync when we did have a mission. The farm was a fortified base, so it seemed logical to turn it into a government safe house. It provided us the opportunity to keep us on our toes with our training and to experiment with new technology. I guess you could say it gave us something to do in between missions to Vietnam."

"Why did you go back to Vietnam the other day?"

"Wentworth needed the base destroyed. He was going to send Max and Zach to do it. That base was heavily booby trapped. Only The Ghosts knew where they all were and how to deactivate the homemade devices. The guys would've been killed. I couldn't let that happen. There was also no way Jack was going to let me go back. I had no choice, but to do what I did.

"Jack never wanted me to go back to Vietnam. He wanted to bring me to the U.S. and give me a normal life. It's nine years later, and he's finally gotten his wish. The only problem is that I don't know if I can live a normal life. I feel very lost right now. That's what worries him. That's why he wants someone with me at all times. He's worried I'm going to lose control of myself.

"I know you care about me. I have feelings for you too. You need to know that I don't know if I can lead a normal life, give you what you dream to have. I may be unpredictable, and do some unusual things. I might even be crazy. I understand if you don't want that uncertainty."

Mark pulled her into his arms. "I've been through quite a few unusual things with Billy." He smiled at her. "I love you, Sam. I'm here for you in any capacity that you need me."

Sam leaned her head into his chest, giving him a long, tight hug. When she finally pulled back, her lips met his and they kissed for an extended period of time.

"Since you're helping babysit me, why don't we take that trip to Hawaii that you've always dreamed of?"

"You're serious?" Mark could see a gleam in her eyes as his body filled with excitement.

"Why not? Are you up to the task of teaching me how to live a normal life?"

Their trip to Hawaii was more amazing than Mark could have ever dreamed. Not only did he finally get to see the place, but he shared it with the woman he loved. It was two weeks that were the most incredible of his entire life. Unfortunately, it couldn't last. Rick needed him back in L.A. to help with a new client; and General Wentworth needed Sam in Washington, D.C. While she was there, Sam was going to start working on getting him pardoned.

The separation was hard, but unavoidable. They would try to talk on the phone twice a week, but their different schedules didn't always allow for that to happen. Mark missed her terribly.

Weeks turned into months. Mark and Rick were arrested and put on military trial. Mark kept hoping to see Sam. She was all he thought about. He wanted to see her one more time before he faced the "firing squad". Finally, he had a visitor. It was Keyla. She told him Sam was in Genevieve at a U.N. conference with General Wentworth. She had never stopped trying to get them pardoned. Mark asked Keyla to tell Sam 'thank you' and more importantly, tell Sam he loved her with all his heart. Keyla told him she would, and that Sam had never stopped loving him. Sam had a present she wanted to give Mark. Keyla had reached behind her neck, took off a silver, butterfly necklace, and placed it around his neck. She told him Sam was wearing the one he gave her. Mark grabbed Keyla and hugged her. Tears were in his eyes. "Thank you."

They escaped prison with help from General Hawkins. They knew Hawkins from Nam. He was the commanding officer of Lt.Col. Williams. Williams was the one who gave them the orders to deliver the military intel to the South Vietnamese. The mission had gone exactly as planned. They met the guy and delivered the intel. When they returned to base, they were arrested for committing treason. Williams denied giving the orders and accused them of working for the Viet Cong. They had never figured out who set them up or why.

They didn't like working for the general, but he had promised he could get them a pardon if they went on a certain number of suicide missions for him. Rick figured Hawkins knew the truth and wondered what part he had played in everything. They were all skeptical that Hawkins would hold up his end of the bargain, but this could get the pardon they desperately wanted. One positive was that Billy was released from the V.A. and now lived with them.

Virginia

Mark was watching the news one night when a story came on that caught his attention. It was about a bank robbery in Atlanta. It seemed that a young woman, who was being held hostage inside, single-handedly shot all five gunmen and saved all the hostages. Mark smiled at the footage inside the bank. The woman was then shown being stopped and interviewed. "I just did what anyone else would do. I had to stop them from killing everyone." She modestly commented and then was ushered away by Jack. Sam looked more beautiful than he remembered. Mark loved getting to see her, but his heart also ached. He missed her so much.

A few minutes later, Billy walked into the house and announced that he had brought company. He stepped aside, and Mark found himself looking at Sam.

Chapter 16

"Hey, Kid." Rick greeted her. "You're all over the news."

"Yes, that's unfortunate. The footage inside the bank somehow was leaked out. I've had to go into hiding until this blows over."

Mark was still stunned she was there. He walked over to her. "You can stay with us."

"I'm sorry I didn't make it to your trial."

"You had more important things to do." Mark pulled her into his arms. "May I?"

"Please do." She had the biggest, most beautiful smile.

He kissed her deeply, passionately. It had been over seven months since they had seen each other, seven long months.

Mark saw the team start to sweep the place for any new listening bugs Hawkins may have snuck in.

"How's college going?" Rick inquired.

"Not good," Sam replied. "We're having a hard time relating to what they are teaching, and we don't understand half of the English that is being spoken. Jack and Simon try to help us at home, but neither of them went to college. Keyla tried to translate during class, but we got into trouble for talking. I've never felt so frustrated before. One day, I lost it and took a machine gun to the barn. After that, Jack installed some punching bags for us. Chang heads for them as soon as we're home." She smiled. "We've given them names. Shakespeare gets beaten on the most and has been replaced several times already.

"It is so important to Jack that we graduate. I don't want to disappoint him. However, we're failing four of our classes. The only reason we're passing Biology is because Graham can explain it in ways we understand. And music, that one's easy. If I could just wrap my head around it, I could teach it to the others."

"I'll help you." Mark offered.

"We'll all help you." Rick added. "We all went to college. Give each of us a subject."

"Thank you."

Mark took Economics, a subject that came naturally to him. He thoroughly enjoyed explaining all the concepts in terms of Vietnam. They spent the entire remainder of the afternoon together. It was magical.

At dinner, Rick gave them a lesson in world religions in military terms. Mark couldn't believe she was actually there. He kept squeezing her hand or hugging her.

The following day, he took her out for lunch. They used some of Rick's props to conceal her identity. It was nice to get off the compound and out from under Hawkins' prying eyes. The team wasn't going to tell anyone, especially Hawkins, who she really was.

Mark learned that she was going to college in Atlanta with Keyla, Chang, Won, and My. Currently, they were taking their classes together from 8am until 1pm Monday, Wednesday, and Friday. On Tuesday and Thursday, the Lihn Ma flew to Paris Island, S.C. to train Marines. Those were her favorite days, especially when they got to be the enemy and shoot people with paint guns. Sam and Jack had come to an understanding, she could continue helping General Wentworth, but no more combat missions. This had several benefits including using her rank to access key government documents. She had also learned how to swap favors with the top brass. However, getting their pardon was full of roadblocks; success wasn't looking promising.

When they returned from lunch, Hawkins was in the house.

"Lieutenant, it's time for your friend to leave. You have a new mission." Hawkins told him.

Mark wrapped his arms around Sam's waist. "Whatever you have to say to me, you can say in front of Sam."

"I don't think so. She leaves now." Hawkins told him in his usual arrogant, pompous tone.

"Sam's not leaving, so I guess we're not going on a mission."

"Oh well, no mission." Rick said and the team started going back to what they had been doing before Hawkins arrived.

Mark just grinned at Hawkins, holding Sam tightly in his arms. Hawkins was a bully who controlled their lives. Today, he was not going to be given the right to take Sam away.

Hawkins conceded and let Sam in on the meeting. His refusal to take any responsibility if anything happened to her, wasn't a surprise. It was a mission to Italy; Sam was keen to go.

Italy

It was wonderful being in Rome pretending to be on his honeymoon with Sam; a romantic couple's getaway. This was by far the best plan Rick had ever had. Mark just wished it could be real, but he had decided he wasn't going to marry her as a criminal. She deserved better.

They were visiting all the big tourist sites in a particular order, so their contact could spot them. All was going smoothly until they were standing in front of the Fontana di Trevi. Sam suddenly looked to him and said. "What if I can't do normal?"

"You've been doing a great job so far." He pulled her into his arms. "What's wrong?"

"I've never been around so many people. I don't understand what they are saying. We are in this tiny square surrounded by all these buildings and windows; we're sitting ducks out here. People are bumping into me and some of them have guns. I want to neutralize them."

"The people here are tourist from all over the world. No one wants to hurt you. Nobody knows who you are. As for the people with the guns, let's keep an extra eye out for them and tell Rick what they look like. The team has us covered. You have to act normal. It's almost time to walk down the little side street and find the pizza shop where we pick up the microfiche." He smiled at her. She still looked uneasy. "Hey, you can do this. I'm going to be right by your side the entire time. I'm going to help you through this, just follow my lead." He leaned in to kiss her. Mark knew how hard she was trying to be normal; unlike fighting, it didn't come naturally to her. He also knew he could seduce her to act normal when he kissed her; she loved his kisses.

(Hawkins)

Virginia

A helicopter suddenly landed on the lawn. He watched as several people jumped out and ran toward the house. Hawkins rotated his chair to face his computer monitor turning on visual and audio inside the house.

Sam, the girl Lt. Luce took on one of their missions, walked into the house followed by a guy carrying some boxes, two young Vietnamese men, and a young Vietnamese woman.

"The Ghosts have landed." Billy commented.

The man carrying the boxes started setting them up.

"I came as fast as I could, Rick." Sam told him. "What can you tell me?"

"We don't know much. Mark was taken by a guy last night while he and Billy were in town. He was a Hispanic man around five foot five. Billy thought he heard the name Miguel Pablo. That's it. We told Hawkins, but he isn't doing anything to help us. We've been out all night looking, but the trail is completely cold."

"Zach, run the name Miguel Pablo though the system. Tell me if you find anything."

A few moments passed. "Got it. Boy, this is one mean guy. Take a look."

Sam looked at the monitor, but Hawkins couldn't see it. He had run the name himself and there was no such person.

"This guy is a serious drug runner. I wonder what he wants with Mark."

"Why didn't Hawkins give us this information?" Rick asked.

"His security clearance isn't high enough." She smiled.

Hawkins was annoyed. Just who exactly was she and how could she possibly have a security clearance higher than his? She was just a young girl in her twenties.

"Track him, Zach."

"He's in Santa Marta, Columbia"

"Mark has a tracker?" Rick inquired.

"Yes. The more I heard about Hawkins; the more I distrusted him. I was worried he was just going to abandon you guys someplace terrible or hide you away in a secret prison. The last time I was here, I gave Mark one of my tracking devices. He's activated the signal."

"Sam, we have an incoming call from General Wentworth."

"Put him through."

Hawkins didn't like this piece of information. General Ben Wentworth was an enemy of his. They had crossed paths and butted heads many times during their military careers. They both worked "inside the system", and Wentworth had foiled some of Hawkins's plans in the past. This was something Hawkins was never going to forget or forgive. Which really begged the question, who was Sam?

"Sam, it's been brought to my attention that you just signed off on the entire unit suddenly taking a leave of absence. What's going on?" Wentworth inquired.

"A Columbian drug lord has kidnapped Mark. We're going to rescue him."

"Sam, I'm sorry, but I'm not going to be able to allow this. All leave is hereby denied."

Hawkins smiled. He didn't like Wentworth, but for once he agreed with him.

Wentworth continued, "Instead, this is an official mission with full resources. Sam, go get Lieutenant Luce and bring him home safely."

She smiled. "Thank you."

Hawkins was furious. Who was Wentworth to move in on his action?

Billy entered the room with the Vietnamese people. "We've packed everyone's bags. We're ready to go."

"Great! We're going to Columbia." Sam looked at Rick. "You ready?"

Rick motioned his hand for her to go first. "Lead the way, Kid."

They quickly rushed out of the house, onto the chopper, and took off. Hawkins was fuming. Leaving the compound to go on their own private missions was strictly prohibited. They were going to have to go on an extra mission for him as a punishment.

The following morning, Hawkins received a video call from Rick. When he answered it, he found himself looking at the entire team dressed in their Army dress uniforms. They were standing on some sort of yacht. They were all facing Sam, who was wearing a Marine Corps. uniform. Hawkins looked closely at the uniform and realized that Sam was a brigadier general. A terrible feeling suddenly came over him.

"Major Richard Peters, Capt. Billy Baxter, and Lt. Mark Luce," Sam said, "On behalf of the Pentagon and the President of the United States, it is with great honor and pleasure that I hereby pardon you. Congratulations!" She smiled.

They saluted her; she saluted back. Sam then walked over and shook each of their hands. When she got to Mark, he grabbed her in his arms and they kissed.

Hawkins was furious. Now that they were pardoned, he no longer could use them for his private missions.

Rick walked up to the camera providing the live feed. "We'll be back in a few weeks to get our things out of your house." He laughed. "See ya, Hawkins."

The screen then went blank.

(Mark)

Saint John, U.S. Virgin Islands

Mark kissed Sam again. This was the happiest day of his life. Not only had he finally been pardoned, but Sam had been allowed to do it. Now, they were free to focus on their next mission, which required a change of clothes.

An hour later, the team was standing back on the deck again, but this time, they were all wearing tuxedos. Mark couldn't remember ever feeling this nervous. The music started playing and there she was, on Jack's arm, dressed in white. Sam looked absolutely gorgeous.

Kelly officiated.

Mark kissed the bride. The plan really had come together nicely. His fake kidnapping, which Billy and General Wentworth were in on, to get the team away from Hawkins. The conning of the yacht down on St. John's, that was big enough to hold Sam's extended family. The pardon Sam got signed by President

Jimmy Carter giving them their freedom. Yes, they were finally free. What a great word it was, 'free'; free of Hawkins, free of being on the run, free to live a normal life.

The next two weeks yachting around the Caribbean with their friends, was going to be a great start to their new life. They were going to go snorkeling numerous times, enjoy lounging in the sun, and Sam was going to be free to wear anything she wanted without worrying about strangers seeing her scars and questioning who she was.

Mark had asked Sam how she pulled off their pardon. She simply told him that she asked The President and he said "yes". However, five months after their marriage, the farm went on lockdown, because Air Force One was landing. Mark quickly discovered that it wasn't The President's first time to UTAH.

UTAH

Shortly after that, Rick came to visit. He asked Sam a question that had been on his mind. "Sam, that night in the hangar, I've always had a strange feeling something else was happening."

"Let's just say I'm glad I was right about all of you."

Mark's curiosity was peaked. "What if you hadn't been right?"

Sam looked away.

"Sam, please tell me."

She looked back toward them, but Mark could see the distance in her eyes. "The Ghosts had you surrounded. Chang was behind you with his gun aimed and ready to fire. Won and My had the flanks. They were waiting for my order. If you hadn't agreed to keep my secret, they would have fired and hit you with tranq darts. We would have loaded you and your van into The Beluga, and flown you back to L.A.. Graham would have hit you with a drug that would have erased all memory of me, my family, and this farm. You would have woken up confused, but safe.

"I had already buried Walters; he knew who I was. I had General Harris put a gag order on him and assign him a desk job. I tried to bury your file, but you guys had annoyed quite a few people in the Army, and Harris decided to personally go after you."

As the reality of what could have happened hit Mark, he gave Sam a hug. "I'm glad you were right about us."

She smiled, "Me too."

Did they live happily ever after? You could say that. The farm continued to be a top secret military safe house; the Underground Tactical Assault Hideout. Sam always enjoyed getting her family back together to protect the farm. What exactly her role was with the government, Mark never knew and didn't ask. He guessed she was CIA.

As far as children went, they weren't able to have any of their own. They think it was due to Agent

Orange exposure. However, since they were both orphans, they opened a children's home to prevent siblings from being separated. The farm made a great home for the seven children they raised over the years with Jack's help. Whenever the farm went on lockdown, the kids stayed with their Uncles Scott and Graham.

Billy moved to the farm, helped with the children, and taught private flying lessons off their runway. Rick traveled around the U.S. for a bit. While he was hiking in Bryce Canyon National Park, he met a woman and they eventually married.

The legend of the Ghost Soldiers eventually started to fade away as all things do with time. But for those who were rescued by them; they'll never been forgotten.

About the Author:

Shawn Settle spent most of her childhood in the coastal town of Wilmington, NC; and graduated from Wake Forest University. As an adult, she has lived in five different states and also abroad, in Australia. She has been writing since she was in the third grade; and is currently an elementary teacher in San Antonio, TX, teaching underprivileged children. She is an avid traveler and cross-stitcher. Her summers are spent traveling around the U.S. with her family; her goal of visiting all 50 states was accomplished in June 2017. It's not uncommon for places she has visited to show up in her stories.

About the Illustrator:

Amanda Bonner lives in San Antonio, Texas, and has been drawing for most of her life. She loves digital art, reading, and horseback riding. After school, her dream is to become a toy designer.

Made in the USA
Columbia, SC
09 August 2017